THE
KEY TO
EVERY
THING

THE
KEY TO
EVERY
THING

PAT SCHMATZ

CANDLEWICK PRESS

First edition 2018

Library of Congress Catalog Card Number pending
ISBN 978-0-7636-9566-8

18 19 20 21 22 23 LSC 10 9 8 7 6 5 4 3 2 1

Printed in Crawfordsville, IN, U.S.A.

This book was typeset in Berkeley.

Candlewick Press
99 Dover Street
Somerville, Massachusetts 02144

visit us at www.candlewick.com

HEY, DIANE!
THIS IS FOR YOU.

PART ONE

EVERYTHING

IS

DIFFERENT

NOW

Morning sunbeams streamed through the window. Tasha closed her eyes and turned away.

"You up?" Her great uncle Kevin knocked, then opened the bedroom door. "Awake?"

Tasha nodded without opening her eyes.

"Time to get up," said Kevin. "We're leaving in twenty minutes."

He closed the door. Tasha rolled out of bed and got dressed. She kept her back to the window that faced the Captain's Quarters next door. If Cap'n Jackie was watching for a morning salute, she'd have to wait a long, long time.

Tasha passed Kevin in the hall on the way to the bathroom. She did not speak. She refused breakfast. When he said it was time to go, she picked up her heavy backpack and followed him out the door of their second-floor apartment. She trudged down the stairs behind him and out the back door of the duplex. As they crossed the backyard, she didn't even glance sideways at the leafy tunnel through the hedge to Cap'n Jackie's.

Tasha opened the passenger door of Terkel, Kevin's battered brown Tercel. She flipped the seat forward and crawled behind it, fastened her seat belt, and crossed her arms.

"Bug." Kevin leaned into the passenger side door. His usually longish hair was buzzed short for his trip, leaving his forehead pale and bare. He hardly even looked like Kevin. "It's a seven-hour drive. You're not really going to backseat it the whole way, are you?"

Tasha stared straight ahead. She was nobody's bug.

"All right, then, have it your way." He clicked the front seat into place and eased the passenger door closed. Rounding Terkel, he folded his lanky body into the driver's seat. "That means I choose the music all day."

Tasha stared straight ahead.

"If you want to apologize to Cap'n Jackie before we go, I'm happy to wait." Kevin turned to look at her. "I don't know what all you said last night, but I'm thinking it wasn't good."

No, it wasn't good. But even if Tasha was sorry—and she wasn't, well, mostly not—Cap'n Jackie wouldn't change her mind. Neither of them would.

"That woman loves you with her whole heart. You know we couldn't get along without her."

Tasha thought maybe she could. Maybe. She'd never thought that before, but she thought it now.

"It's not her fault, you know."

Tasha turned away, looking out the passenger window. There was no point in arguing. Kevin and Cap'n Jackie were teamed up against her, and they wouldn't listen to anything she said.

"Okay." He turned back around and started the car. "Stay mad if you need to. But eventually you'll do the right thing. I know you."

If he really knew her, he'd forget his stupid selfish trip to New Zealand and stay home for a normal summer. He'd send Grandfather McCorry's money back with a big No Thank You.

Instead, he backed out of the driveway and into the alley. Terkel rolled into the street and headed for the freeway.

Tasha was done talking, but that didn't stop the words from rolling around in her head. They rolled right along with the hum of the tires on the highway.

They both suck. Suck suck suck. They don't care about me. Kevin only cares about stupid New Zealand. It's probably not even a camp he's taking me to. It's probably an orphanage or a work camp or worse. Something sinister. A friggin' Croc pit or something.

Even if it is just a stupid camp, they're still banishing me. They think I'll come home and everything will be the same again. Well, you know what? It won't. It'll never be the same again. Not after throwing the key. And I didn't even mean to.

Why does that stupid key have to be such a big deal, anyway? It doesn't even open anything. I don't need a fake magic key. I just need to stay home with Cap'n Jackie. So what if she can't cook?

"I can't feed you for a whole month. You'd starve."

"We could have pizza. I'll make grilled cheese."

"You can't live on cheese."

"I'd eat a carrot every single day. And an apple. I'd be fine. We could work on the Home Alone project and watch movies and play Parcheesi and order pineapple on our pizza."

"What happens when you pitch your eighty-seventh rager? And I pitch one back? And there's no Kevin to come home and separate us?"

"I won't. I won't pitch a single rager."

"I need my downtime."

"When you need downtime I'll go in my room and be quiet."

"You can argue all day and all night, my Kid. The decision's been made."

"Unmake it!"

"It's not mine to unmake. You're going to do some growing up this summer. You'd best get started on it."

"You just don't want me."

"Nonsense. Stand up and take it on the chin."

Okay, so I shouldn't have thrown the key, and I shouldn't have called her a crazy old lady or said suck. But it's not fair. None of it's fair. They think they can push me around because I'm a kid. So fine. Push me around. But you can't make me be nice about it.

I won't.

Twice for no.

No. No.

"Bug. You awake?"

Tasha peeled her sticky eyes open. They were in a parking lot. The sun was high and hot. She looked out the window and read the sign. KOUNTRY KRITTERS KAFE.

"No."

"You have to eat something."

"I'm not hungry."

"You need to eat. I can't drop you off at camp like a starving junkyard dog."

"Since when do you care? All you care about is New Zealand."

Kevin sighed and turned to face the front.

"Look," he said. "You're right. I do care about New Zealand. But it's not just that. I really do think this can be good for you. You know that. In your heart of hearts, you know it."

Tasha rolled her eyes up to Terkel's ceiling. She shouldn't have talked. Now he'd blahblah for hours about how great camp was and how great it was when he was a kid and how great it was that Grandfather McCorry was paying for it all.

Blahblah. No more talking.

Kevin made her go into the Kountry Kritters Kafe (who thought of *that* name?) and he ordered her a grilled cheese sandwich and fries and a shake that she did not touch, although she wanted to, but that would be acting like everything was okay and everything was *not* okay. Kevin ate a burger and blahblahed between bites. Tasha stared at the red-and-white-checked tablecloth.

The drive to camp took forever, but suddenly they were turning off the freeway, under trees, onto a dirt road. Squirmy little twisters woke up in Tasha's stomach. Good thing she hadn't eaten that lunch or she'd be barfing all over Terkel. Then Kevin would be sorry. Maybe she should have eaten. Kevin wouldn't leave a barfing kid behind, would he?

Tasha was still thinking about barfing when Kevin introduced her to the camp director. She nodded hello, but she did not open her mouth. Same with the counselor. Tasha did not speak as Kevin carried her trunk and set it next to a bunk bed.

"Maddie!" A skinny girl with a single long braid

ran from the other side of the little cabin and threw her arms around another kid who was just coming in. "Oh my God, oh my God, we're in Hinky Haven!"

Screaming laughter. Jumping up and down. Kevin made Tasha's bed, tucked her pajamas under the pillow, and led her out the door. They walked away from the cabins and the cars and the people and the noise. He stopped under a big tree next to a tennis court.

"Tasha." Kevin dropped to one knee and turned her to face him. "Tasha, look at me."

She did and then wished she hadn't. Behind his glasses, Kevin's hazel eyes were shiny and swimmy. A tear fell out, and he brushed a knuckle across his cheek to catch it.

"You're making this really hard."

Good. Why should it be easy for him?

"I love you, my Bug. You're my best."

He hugged her and she didn't hug him back. He would change his mind. He would. No way would Kevin leave her.

But he did. He got in Terkel and he drove away. Out of habit, Tasha reached in her pocket for the key.

It wasn't there. It was probably still lying on Cap'n Jackie's kitchen floor.

July 17

Dear Kid,

Okay, silent treatment is over. But you hurt my feelings, you know. I didn't mind the crazy or old so much, but lady? Crazy old lady? That was just mean.

And the key? Like I told you four years ago, if you can't take care of it then you don't get to keep it.

Kevin deserves that trip to New Zealand and you know it. Camp for you wasn't my idea, but it's not the worst idea ever. My made-up stories are the best I can offer, and I'm afraid a month of that would bore you. As you pointed out, you are outgrowing all that magic nonsense.

I wish you weren't in such a big stinkin' hurry to grow up. You're right, you don't need a pretend-magic key. You were breathing magic from that first day I saw you hunkered down in my raspberry bush. You can ignore it if you want, but the magic is still there.

Just writing this letter is making me less mad.

Since you're stuck at camp for a month, you might as well enjoy it. Find some friends. If you have a rager attack, go throw some rocks (not at anyone's head). Or draw a picture of the Crocs chewing on my guts and send it to me. I'll put it on the fridge.

When you come back, we'll start Project Home Alone. It'll be good. You'll see.

I love you bigger than any gritty nasty rager storm you can ever throw at me. And that's pretty dang big.

Now and Forever,
Captain Jackie

July 18

Dear Bug,

By the time you get this, you're probably loving camp already. I'm leaving for the airport in a few minutes and I'll drop this in the mailbox on the way.

I hope you've written to Cap'n Jackie and apologized. If you haven't, do it soon. Like now. And send your grandfather a thank-you letter. You know I'll hear about it if you don't. It doesn't have to be long and you don't have to mean it. Just do it.

I bet you have a favorite horse. Maybe you've been water-skiing. I can't wait to get my first e-mail from you. I want to hear all about everything. Every single thing.

Love,
Your Great! Uncle!
aka Your Kevin

11

July 20

Dear Kevin,

   This is so stupid. They won't let me type
the e-mail myself. They make me write to
you with a stupid pen so I can be just like
everyone else and then SOMEONE ELSE types it.
As if I'd break the computer by touching the
preshisss—I know that's not spelled right but
I don't care—keyboard. Just so you know. This
isn't me writing. Someone might be changing my
words that are supposed to be *private*.

   Why can't I use an envelope like all the
other kids? Because my so-called "parent
or guardian" is OUT OF THE COUNTRY and NOT
REACHABLE IN ANY NORMAL WAY even if I DROWN or
GET KICKED IN THE HEAD BY A HORSE or GET LOST
FOREVER IN THE WOODS.

   So anyway. Dear Kevin. This place is full
of mozzies. That's what my counselor calls
them. And deerflies. The deerflies bite really
hard. I already have 47 bites total. 41 mozzies
and 5 deerfly and one I'm not sure. Probably
a spider, black widow or something worse. You
should be worried. It's a huge bite.

Tasha
p.s. I am still mad.

July 21

Dear Kid,

Here are some cookies. Share them around. They have MAGIC powers. Hahaha. Because magic is still real whether you believe it or not. Magic or not, cookies will help you make friends.

Draphin misses you. Her chin drags on the ground and she's all full of sad eyes. She says I shouldn't have let you go. She says I should have kidnapped you and hidden you in the basement until Kevin was on the plane. She can't believe I let you leave without the key. She says you will forget her if you don't have the key.

I told Draphin that you are living in REALITY now.

Reality is not such a bad place to be. Sometimes it's nice. Mulligan lived here in the real world and made it nicer for both of us. So did my Vanessa. Sometimes real is good.

Anyway. I've been enjoying the key. I squeeze it

tight and take long flights with Draphin. We go see vanessa and Mulligan. That key still has plenty of good magic left in it. If you hadn't thrown it AT MY HEAD, you'd know.

Have some real-world fun at that real-world camp. I hope you're riding horses every day.

Just don't forget who's your captain. Or I'll make you walk the plank into a seething mass of Crocs. All different colors of poison pastel. Don't laugh. They are dangerous and you know it.

Love,
Captain Jackie

July 22

Dear Grandfather McCorry,

Thank you for paying for camp. Camp is full of fresh air. If Kevin dies in New Zealand or his plane crashes, don't worry about me. Send a lot of money

14

to our next-door neighbor Jackie Moscato. She'll take care of me until my dad comes home.

Your granddaughter,
Natasha K. McCorry

July 27

Dear Kid,

Seven years today. Seven years since I found a rag-a-nothin in my raspberries. Mulligan meowed at the kitchen window until I looked out back and spotted your little bare toes sticking out from under the brambles.

Poor Kevin. He's a saint, you know. He was charging up and down the alley calling you, tears running down his face. He just about kissed my feet when I turned you over with bandages on your bramble scratches. Said he wasn't fit to take care of a child, losing you the first day. I told him he was. I told him it was Mulligan's fault. He tossed his best black-cat magic into the alley and hooked you and reeled you into our world.

Nathan called me that day. Did you know that? Maybe I told you before, I can't remember. He hadn't called in months, but there he was on the phone that day. He said he woke up thinking about me.

I told him a child just moved in next door. He said you were a lucky child. I thought no, I'm a lucky captain. After two years of me and Mullie wandering around the house in our lonelies, you came in the nick of time. The past seven years have whizzed by like a tornado.

You've been at camp almost two weeks now. Time enough for my package to get there. Did you eat the cookies or not?

Happy friend-a-versary.

Love,
Captain Jackie

July 27

Dear Cap'n Jackie,

You know what? Those cookies weren't magic. They were delischus but not magic. I know that's not how you spell it. You know what I mean. Happy friend-a-versary anyway. Are you having a party without me? Camp is better than I thought it would be. I'm sorry about the key and stuff. Don't go in my room till I get back, okay? Just keep the door closed.

I have friends here. Gwen is my best friend. She is cool. You know what? I told her about my dad and her dad is in prison too! She says lots of dads are but nobody knows because nobody tells. She lives with her mom. I told her I live with Kevin and she didn't even ask me where my mom was. Gwen says one-sillabel names are stronger. She calls me Tash. I like that better.

And guess what? I'm playing Capt

July 27

Dear Kevin,

Happy family-versary. I am Captain Hook in the camp play. Gwen is Peter Pan. Gwen's my best friend. She lives in Chicago.

My favorite horse is Pepper. I fell off of her last week. I have a ginormous bruise on my leg. If I'd broken it and I was in the hospital nobody would come and visit me because you're on the other side of the world and Cap'n Jackie wouldn't leave her house. Don't worry. I'll survive.

I'm glad New Zealand is fun. Really. Mostly really. They print me out your e-mails and give them to me, but it's not the same as a letter in the mail.

If it wasn't for Cap'n Jackie I wouldn't get any mail at all. I have 4 postcards from her and two letters and a package with cookies. I started a sorry letter to her but then I got interrupted and I can't find it. Gwen gets a REAL letter IN AN ENVELOPE in the mail every day. But don't feel guilty or anything.

Gwen and I are going on a horse campout on Saturday.

Sincerely,
TASH—don't call me Bug or Tasha anymore.
I AM TASH.

18

July 31

Dear Kid,

You've been gone forever. I thought you'd send me a howler or a snarler. But nothing? Not even a lousy thank-you for the cookies? Are you giving me the silent treatment? It's lasting too long, and now it hurts as much as your key-throwing fit.

Or . . . maybe it's not the silent treatment.

The times, they are a changing. I knew it from the second Kevin told me about the summer plan. You really are growing up. I will see less and less of you and then you'll be gone. More gone than Vanessa and Mullie, because they are both still in this house with me. I hear them, and sometimes I see a flash of one or the other. Call me crazy — I don't care. Wouldn't be the first time.

No, you'll be gone like Nathan but even more. Because Nathan was ours. When Vanessa's brother kicked him out, we were all he had. We wrapped him in layers of shiny light and launched him off into the world, and look at him now. New York City with his dream job, living the life.

But you, my kid, are not really my kid. I will not be your teen-launcher. You have Kevin for that and he loves you more than any parent ever could. And your dad will be free someday, and he'll be your dad again. I'll be the person of your little childhood, your imagination, and you're leaving me behind. Middle school, friends, camp, sports, a car, dates, college . . . no use trying to drag you back on ship. You're on your way out the door already.

It's more painful than Nathan's move to New York could ever be. For the next few years, you'll be a stone's throw and a million light years away, and then you'll be gone.

Draphin feels it, but as you pointed out, Draphin is MADE UP and there is NO SUCH THING AS A DOLPHIN-DRAGON. Or a dragon-dolphin. You might not believe in Draphin, but she believes in you and she's not sad. She's happy for you because she's

20

magic. Not me. I've got green scales falling like rain.

You'll never see this letter, my kid. I will not send it. Never never, twice for no.

Why?

Because I want you to spread your snarly little wings and fly into the world.

I just wish you didn't have to leave me so far behind.

I saw what you wrote on the wall. I guess you're right. I'm really not the captain of anything.

Still. I wish you'd send me a letter from camp.

Just one.

I'm not even mad anymore.

I'm sad. And I'll never send this letter.

August 1

My Dear Captain, Heart of my Heart,

I did it! I've carved out a weekend to come and see you. I've been a selfish brat, I know, and it's been way way way way way too long.

Almost two years! How did I let that happen?
I feel terrible. But finally, finally, my life is
coming together. The job is amazing, and true
love is the most amazing of all!

Theo asked me to marry him, and I knocked
once for yes! We are officially engaged!!!! I am
bringing him home. You'll adore him. He's strong
and steady and wise and kind. And stable!
I fell in love with someone stable!

We are arriving on Thursday the 4th and
staying until Sunday. Don't worry,
I rented a place nearby so we won't get
in your way. We will bring piles of groceries
and cook a big, beautiful dinner Thursday
night. I bet you haven't eaten right since
Vanessa left us. I'm bringing her recipe box, and
I will cook us up a storm.

We'll leave your freezer stocked with enough
to last until the next time we visit. We plan
to visit a LOT, so you'd better get used to
it. Yes, yes, I'll call before we come. Thursday
afternoon.

22

I can't wait to see you. It's been too long. I know, that's my fault. I just couldn't seem to get myself together. But now I am.

With all of my love,
and then some more,
Nathan

August 1

Dear Cap'n Jackie,
    Thank you for the cookies.
    I haven't had a letter or postcard from you in a while. Are you mad again? I wrote you a letter last week but the bell rang in the middle and then I lost it so now I'm starting over.
    I'm sorry I threw the key. I'm sorry I said you suck. I didn't mean any of it. Don't go in my room, okay? If you already did and you saw what I wrote, I don't mean that either.

I'm Captain Hook in the camp play. I know most of my lines. My best friend Gwen is Peter Pan. We have a sword fight. You'd like the sword fight. Good thing you taught me how to do it and how to walk with a cane.

Gwen is tough. She stays by herself after school for two hours every day before her mom gets home. Being here at camp is not helping me on the Home Alone plan because I'm never alone. When I get home, will you still help me? Why do I have to be such a chicken? I want to be tough and brave like Gwen.

I hope you're having a relaxing summer with lots of downtime. I hope you're not too lonely. If I had to stay alone all summer, I'd go crazy.

I'm sorry I called you a crazy old lady. I was a little stinker. You can call me that right out loud when I get home. I deserve it.

Love,
Tash
I am Tash now. Not Kid. Not Bug. Not Tasha.
Tash.

DREAMING

Cap'n Jackie's house was wrapped in hush. The air lay thick, hot, and humid, but all was quiet like the morning after a snow. Quiet like the morning after Mullie died. Tash's feet made no sound on the floor.

Where was Cap'n Jackie? Upstairs? Downstairs? No sounds anywhere. If Tash hurried, she could paint over the writing on the wall before Cap'n Jackie saw it. It was hard to hurry, though. The dense air wrapped around her legs, slowing her down. It was like running through water. Tash finally reached the door to her room and threw it open.

The wall was gone. Not just the words. The whole wall was open to the world, a different world with black mountains inked against a deep purpling sky.

Suddenly a huge black shadow swooped through the twilight, and Tash jumped back, her heart pounding. What was that? She crept up close to the wall—but it wasn't a wall anymore. It was glass. She pressed her nose against it, searching for the thing that had made the shadow.

There! There it was, soaring high. It crossed the silvery half-moon. Dragon head, broad wings, long fluked tail. Draphin! The enormous creature dove from moon height, spiraling down. Fireflies surrounded her, weaving, lighting her shape, buzzing around her head in a glowing crown.

As Draphin circled closer, a figure took form between her wings. It was Cap'n Jackie. She stood taller than tall on two feet, no cane, arms out, swaying in balance with Draphin's movements. They flew through the moonlight, a gliding dance and spin, perfect grace and motion, closer and closer.

Tash waved with both arms. Draphin swept close to the window again, casting a shadow that dashed across the room. Tash met one enormous indigo eye for a split second, and it saw her, but there was no recognition. Cap'n Jackie didn't even look her way.

Tash knocked on the glass.

"Cap'n Jackie!" She tried to yell, but nothing came out. "Draphin! Wait for me!"

She banged on the window with both fists.

"I didn't mean it!" Why wouldn't her lips move? Why didn't her voice work? "I'm sorry! I didn't mean it!"

Tash jerked awake, sitting up sharp. The camp bed squeaked. She blinked in the early gray light and looked across to the next bunk. Gwen was wrapped around her pillow, sound asleep. In the bottom bunk, Maya snored softly.

Tash lay back and closed her eyes. She hoped Cap'n Jackie had the sorry letter by now. She wished she'd sent it sooner.

PART TWO

ALONE

"Bug."

Kevin's voice.

"Wake up, baby. We're home."

Not just the voice. Kevin. Unstrapping her seat belt.

"Come on. You're too big for me to carry."

Tash lifted her heavy head, moved her heavy legs. Stood on her sleepy feet and leaned against Terkel's hood. Kevin reached in back and got her backpack, then closed the door quietly. The asphalt still radiated the day's heat. The dark was heavy and damp, split by the streetlight in the alley.

"We'll get your trunk in the morning."

No lights were on at Cap'n Jackie's.

"What time is it?" Tash asked.

"Eleven thirty," said Kevin. "Late."

Tash followed him across the dark yard. He unlocked the side door and pushed it open. He put his finger to his lips, and they tiptoed past the door to the downstairs apartment. The stairwell felt foreign to Tash, as if she'd been gone forever. The dense, close air was so different from the open piney breezes of the past four weeks. Kevin unlocked their door, and Tash followed him through the kitchen to her own bedroom.

"Get in bed, my Bug. I'll be in to kiss you good night in a few minutes."

"Tash," said Tash. "Not Bug."

"Tash."

Kevin kissed her forehead and left the room. Tash unzipped the pocket of her backpack and pulled out the plastic bag. She opened it and sucked in the scent of the lake and morning dip and bare feet in the mud.

"Keep this to remember me by."

Tash and Gwen had snuck down to the lake that morning before the wake-up bell for one last squish of mud through their toes. The rising sun fired red behind the trees. A single red-winged blackbird tweedled from the reedy swamp, and Gwen handed Tash a lake goober from the weedy side next to the swimming area.

Tash put the still-damp goober on her dresser. She pulled clean pj's from her drawer and slid into bed. Her bed felt good, smooth and cool. So very quiet. No pillow tossing or squeaky bunk beds, no whispers or snorts or giggles. How could she be in two such different worlds, all in the same day?

"Tash?"

Kevin sat on the edge of her bed and smoothed back her hair. He was Kevin all right. His hair had grown back in some, not quite normal but getting there.

"You really are Tash now, aren't you?"

"Yes."

"Well, get some sleep. Early shift tomorrow."

Tash had been thinking a lot on the drive home, before she fell asleep. About being grown. About things being different.

"I'll get myself up tomorrow," she said.

"Four thirty a.m.," he reminded her. "It'll still be dark."

"I know. Don't wake me up."

For seven years Kevin had trundled her over to the Captain's house on the early shift days. Even after she was too big to carry, he walked her over half-asleep. Most days she barely remembered the transition and woke in her room at Cap'n Jackie's a couple of hours later.

"Are you sure?" asked Kevin.

"I'm starting middle school in a few weeks."

Kevin brought his eyebrows together in a worry-squinch, deepening the line in the middle.

"You wanted me to grow up, didn't you?" Tash asked.

"Are you sure?"

"Stop saying that."

"All right." Kevin nodded. "I'll call the Captain in the morning and let her know you'll be over later on your own. But grown or not, call me as soon as you get there."

"I should have my own phone, you know. For safety."

"You're right," said Kevin. "I'll look into getting us a landline this week."

"It'd be cheaper to just put me on your plan," Tash said. "With Internet."

34

Kevin knocked the nightstand twice for no. Tash hit it once, raising her own eyebrows.

"Please? Please yes?"

"Talk to me when you're thirteen."

Kevin switched the light off, kissed her forehead again, and closed the door on his way out. Tash rolled to the side of the bed and pushed her window open. The Captain always had lights out by nine, but sometimes she was still up.

"Hey!" Tash whisper-yelled. "Cap'n Jackie! Are you awake?"

No reply. Well, no wonder. It was the middle of the night. Still, seemed like she might have waited up. After all, Tash had been gone for a whole month.

Maybe she was mad that Tash hadn't sent the sorry letter sooner. Well, she'd give Cap'n Jackie a triple-sorry-sorry-sorry in the morning and make everything okay. She'd walk the pretend plank or wash the dishes or scrub the galley floor. Or offer to polish Draphin's muddy front toe-claws. Whatever.

Quiet. So, so quiet. Tash sat up with a start. Not camp. Home. But where was Kevin? Why hadn't he . . . ?

Oh. Right. She was getting herself up.

"I'M FINE." Tash spoke to the silence. "I am. I'm FINE."

She could do this. Gwen stayed alone all the time, for *hours*. Tash scrambled out of bed. Her heart pounded as she opened her bedroom door and checked the kitchen. Nobody there. She took a quick run through the apartment. Nobody there.

She dressed in a hurry and put her house key around her neck, locked their apartment door behind her, and thudded barefoot down the stairs. The downstairs people would be gone to work by now. Tash pulled the back door closed and locked the dead bolt.

Outside, the morning sun stretched across the yard, and the sky was already bright blue. Tash had done it! She'd gotten up and out of the house on her own. First time ever. The Captain would be impressed.

A high hedge separated the backyards, and Kevin had pruned a tunnel so Tash could quick-crawl between yards without getting all scratched up. She dropped to her knees and skittled through, popped out the other side, and shot her arms up as if she'd just landed a perfect ten.

Nobody was there to see it. The back porch was

empty. Tash had thought for sure the Captain would be there, waiting and watching. She high-stepped through the long grass. Drippy morning dew soaked her feet. In the garden, the lettuce was bolting and weeds were popping up everywhere. Tash stopped and stared at the green ragged invaders. Cap'n Jackie must be saving all of the work for her.

She left wet footprints on the worn wood of the porch steps. The back door was closed. Closed! And the shade was drawn! Tash pulled the screen door open and grabbed the doorknob. Locked. Tash jiggled it back and forth.

This was all very strange. Cap'n Jackie never locked that back door, not one time. Tash backed away from the door, looking to the upstairs window. It was closed. Cap'n Jackie didn't close her windows unless it was pouring rain. Sometimes not even then.

Maybe it was a game. Tash rapped the secret knock on the back door. Two thuds with the side of her fist and then three sharp knuckle taps. *THUD. THUD. Tap-ta-tap. THUD. THUD. Tap-ta-tap.*

No answer. She put her ear to the door, a deep unease worming into her stomach. She rapped again. *THUD. THUD. Tap-ta-tap. THUD. THUD. Tap-ta-tap.*

Nothing.

Tash knocked louder, slamming the door until her fist and knuckles hurt. If it was anyone else, Tash would think they'd gone out, but Cap'n Jackie never went out. Kevin called it agoraphobic. Cap'n Jackie had snorted when Tash told her that and said she was idiot-a-phobic and Dr. Kevin could keep his diagnosis to himself. Either way, she never left her yard. Nathan's friend Michael delivered her groceries. Tash or Kevin ran errands for her. She was always home. Always.

So why didn't she answer?

DESPERATE

MEASURES

Maybe Cap'n Jackie was sick. One time last winter they'd gone in and she wasn't in the kitchen like usual. Kevin and Tash took tea and juice up to the Captain's Quarters and Cap'n Jackie didn't come down until later. She spent the day on the couch and made Tash bring her toast with jam and wash the dishes. Probably she was sick again.

But why was the door locked? Why were the windows closed?

Maybe a burglar came and bopped Cap'n Jackie on the head and stole everything. But why would a burglar shut the window and lock the door?

Tash walked around to the front of the house. The yard was completely private, with the hedge on one side and a high fence surrounding the rest. Tash checked the front door and the wooden gate. Both locked, same as always. Returning to the back porch, she tried that door again. Still locked.

Tash stared at the door, chewing her lip. If only she had the real key. She pulled her fingers into a fist, remembering how it felt in her palm. The key was small and solid but slightly bent, as if it had been run over or maybe melted in a fire. Vanessa had given it to Cap'n Jackie long before Tash was even born, and Cap'n Jackie had given it to Tash.

"You put this in your pocket. Keep it there. When you need some magic, squeeze it tight. Draphin and Mulligan and I will have your back, and we'll take care of whatever's going on together. You won't be alone."

The Captain had put the key in Tash's hand and closed her fingers over it. She'd wrapped Tash's little fist in her two big ones and squeezed tight so Tash could feel the warm solid shape of the key press into her skin. It made the badness of Tash's day vanish— swoosh, gone. No more bad, only good.

Tash had carried the key with her every day since,

almost three years now. It was secret. She'd never even told Kevin. He'd picked it up off her nightstand once when he was tucking her in, looked closely and set it back down. He never asked.

Cap'n Jackie had said the key could work in surprising ways. It was an old-style skeleton key, not the kind to open a back door, but maybe it would work in this surprising way. Or maybe somehow this was all about keys. A test? A welcome-home key mystery?

Tash picked up the welcome mat and looked under it, hoping for a clue. Nothing there. She tried her own house key. It slid into the keyhole but didn't turn.

She cupped her hands around her face and tried to look through the blinds into the kitchen. She couldn't see a thing. She stood with her forehead against the window as the *alone* feeling crept up her spine. Kevin said the alone feeling was because of before, when Tash's daddy used to leave her alone a lot. He said now it was an irrational fear, like Cap'n Jackie's agoraphobia.

She and Cap'n Jackie were supposed to practice this summer. Tash would stay at Cap'n Jackie's alone while the Captain went for a stroll down the alley. They'd practice a little at a time. But that all got wrecked with the camp thing and the New Zealand thing.

Tash thumped her forehead against the window. Cap'n Jackie must be in there. Napping, maybe? Or maybe sick. Maybe she needed help.

If Draphin was *real*, a real thing and not a made-up thing, Tash would call her in right this second and ask her to break the door down. No. No, this wasn't a game and the made-up dragon-dolphin would not open the door. This was reality. Something was wrong, definitely wrong. Tash was grown now, and she had to act grown.

Desperate times call for desperate measures.

Cap'n Jackie had said that one time when she and Tash launched a cutlery attack on the Crocs in the backyard. They'd used every piece of silverware in the house, hurling them into the Croc pit until every Croc was . . .

Reality, Tash. Forget about the dang Crocs.

Tash ran down the steps to the side-yard rock garden. She grabbed a rock bigger than her fist, ran back up the steps, and tapped the rock on the lower left square of glass. The glass rattled in its frame. Tash tapped harder. The glass was tough.

It was going to make a lot of noise when it broke. Tash looked around—nobody in sight, of course—and took off her T-shirt. She wrapped it around the rock so it wouldn't be so loud. She thunked it against the glass.

The shirt muffled the noise, but the glass held strong. She stood back a little and hit it again, harder. Nothing. Tash moved in for a better angle, closed her eyes, and hit the rock on the window as hard as she could.

Who knew that little window would be so tough? She unwrapped the shirt and put it back on. Turning her face away, she smacked the glass with all of her might. It was LOUD, but it didn't break. Maybe it was some kind of special burglar-proof glass.

Tash took two steps back, wound up, and side-armed the rock into the window.

CRASH!

WHAT

IF . . .

One shard of glass stuck straight up. Tash eased it out of the frame and set it on the porch next to the door, then reached in and turned the lock on the doorknob. She pushed the door open and looked down at the broken glass, and at her bare feet.

"Cap'n Jackie!" she called from the threshold. "Are you here?"

Cap'n Jackie's old sneakers, the red Chucks that Kevin and Tash had given her for her birthday a few years back, were under the bench on the porch. Tash pulled them out, slid her bare feet in, and stepped into the kitchen, standing on broken glass.

"Cap'n Jackie? It's me, Tash."

The refrigerator hummed. Tash shuffled through the glass. On the other side, she slid out of the shoes and turned them to face the door. She might have to run out in a hurry.

She tiptoed across the hardwood dining-room floor and onto the living-room rug. Everything was quiet and tidy. Sun came in the front window, lighting the short hallway off the dining room. The door to Tash's bedroom was still closed. That was good. Tash pushed it open.

The room was exactly as she'd left it. Tash's writing and drawings and ragings of many years were all over the walls in crayon, marker, and paint. YOU ARE NOT THE CAPTAIN OF ANYTHING was still there, scrawled above her bed in purple Sharpie. Why had she written that? The night-before-camp rager seemed so stupid now, so childish. So Kid, so Bug. So *Tasha*.

Kids at camp joked about their parents moving away while they were at camp and not telling them the new address. What if Cap'n Jackie had moved away? New York, maybe, to live with Nathan? Tash had suspected that maybe Cap'n Jackie loved him best, more than Tash. She had four pictures of Nathan on the wall of the Captain's Quarters. *Four.* And not a single one of Tash.

True, there was a picture of Tash with Mulligan around her neck in the living room. And one in the kitchen. But not *four.* What if the Captain really had moved to New York?

"No." Tash said it out loud. "No, Cap'n Jackie wouldn't do that."

She backed into the hallway and returned to the kitchen, rounding the counter to open the basement door. She peered down into the darkness.

"Cap'n Jackie?"

Alone slithered up the basement steps, and Tash took a step back. She did not like basements. They even smelled lonely. But maybe Cap'n Jackie was down there. Maybe she needed help.

Tash stretched and flipped the light switch. She opened the door as wide as it would go, took three steps down, and squatted to look around. Washer and dryer. Laundry basket. All normal. She listened hard but didn't hear anything beyond the thudding of her own blood in her ears.

She couldn't see behind the furnace or back in the storage room or behind that stack of Nathan's boxes.

46

Come on! Don't be such a chicken.

Just as Tash put her foot on the next step, something gurgled. Tash froze.

Knockitta-clunk. The refrigerator stopped humming. Tash held her breath. What if someone was up there? They could slam the basement door shut and lock it. She'd be down here *forever* because nobody knew where she was and . . .

She dashed back up, closed the basement door behind her, and locked it. She should check the Captain's Quarters. If Cap'n Jackie was sick, that's where she'd be.

"My quarters are off-limits."

That was one of Cap'n Jackie's very strict rules. Tash had only been up there three times in her whole life. Once with Kevin that day when Cap'n Jackie was sick, and two times with Cap'n Jackie.

"Just so you can see there's nothing up here of interest to you."

And there wasn't. Just a bunch of Nathan's art on the wall. And pictures of him and Vanessa. Cap'n Jackie opened closets and drawers to show there was nothing worth snooping. She told Tash that punishment for trespass was eternal banishment to

CrocLand. Tash had never trespassed, not once. Not even when they played hide-and-seek.

Tash knocked on the door to the Captain's Quarters. *THUD. THUD. Tap-ta-tap.* After a long silent pause, she tried again. Then she opened the door and looked up the narrow staircase.

"Cap'n Jackie? You up there?"

Her voice sounded funny. Flat. Hushed. Squished. A little voice in a big empty house. Nobody was up there.

But what if somebody was?

Tash took a big breath and settled her shoulders. She could do this. She started up the stairs, keeping her hand on the railing and watching her feet. What if the stairs suddenly slid out from under her and turned into a slide that sent her slipping down into the basement, down into a secret trap, down into . . .

REALITY, Tash. Reality.

Her heart slammed away, punching like it wanted to get out of her chest. She crept up almost to the top and looked out across the Captain's Quarters. Slowly, she let the breath she'd been holding leak out.

The room was empty. Bed neatly made, spare and quiet.

48

But the bathroom. *Remember that movie? Remember in the bathtub?*

Tash ran up the last couple of steps, across the carpet to the bathroom door. It was slightly ajar. She stood back, out of the center of the doorway, and pushed it open so she could see the tub. It was empty.

"See?" she said. "Nothing. Nobody."

That's right. Nothing and nobody. Just alone. Alone, alone, alone . . .

Tash bolted across the carpet, *thud thud* down the stairs, through the living room. She slipped into the Captain's shoes, *crunch crunch* across the glass, out to the back porch.

She panted as if she'd just run fifteen miles and done twelve push-ups. She wrapped her arms tight around herself, because she was shivering despite the August heat.

Tash sucked in deep breaths of blue-sky air. Kevin. She needed Kevin. If only she had a cell — wait! The landline! She hadn't even thought about it because Cap'n Jackie hardly ever used it.

"Don't you call that a 'landline.' It's a telephone."

She shuffled back up the porch steps and across the glass and picked up the phone. Then she stopped.

49

What if Kevin didn't answer? What if he was gone too? Maybe everybody was. Maybe everyone she knew had been taken to another planet or disappeared or just ran off and left her or —

Tash stopped breathing. Because it could happen. It could. It could happen any time, that every single person you knew disappeared and left you all alone, alone forever . . .

I won't cry. I won't.

Tash hardly ever cried. Sometimes when she raged, water came out of her eyes, but that didn't count. She clenched her teeth to stop them from chattering. What if Cap'n Jackie was really and truly gone? And Kevin, too?

Daddy had five more years to go in prison — practically forever. Grandfather McCorry would stick her in a foster home. He would've before, if Kevin hadn't taken her. Well, Tash wouldn't go. She'd hide.

The quiet alone feeling settled on Tash like a cold mist.

"Stop it!" Tash shook herself like a wet dog. "Get real."

She wiped her nose with the back of her hand and

sniffed hard. Kevin would be there. Kevin was always there. She punched the numbers in before the shivery whisper of doubt had a chance to blow through her bones.

Because what if he wasn't?

ASK

NATHAN

Kevin picked up on the first ring.

"Hi, Cap'n," he said.

"It's me." Tash cleared her throat and got her voice right. "Cap'n Jackie's not here."

"What do you mean she's not there?"

"Not here. I checked everywhere."

Clanking dishes and running water came through the phone line. Kitchen noise from the Biscuit Jam. Tash wished Kevin would say something. Something like, *Oh, I know, I talked to her this morning and* . . .

"Did you check upstairs?" he asked. "And the basement?"

Tash nodded.

"Bug?"

"Yes. I looked everywhere."

"I'm on my way."

As Tash hung up the phone, she blinked to keep the water in. Kevin was coming. He was on his way.

She sat on the back porch and figured how long it would take. Sunday brunch was a busy time, and he might have to finish an order before he left, so it would take until three hundred to finish. Three hundred to get to the car. Five hundred to drive home if she counted slow, so by one thousand one hundred, he should be there. She started at one.

What if he got stopped for speeding? Or got in an accident? She wouldn't worry until two thousand. She was safe until two thousand, especially if she counted slow.

At nine hundred twelve, tires pulled into the next-door driveway. Tash ran across Cap'n Jackie's garden, scooted through the hedge hole, and dashed across the yard. Kevin staggered when she hit him at full speed, but he recovered and scooped her up as if she were five years old.

"I'm here, Bug. I'm right here. We're okay."

He smelled like the Biscuit Jam—baking biscuits and grease and coffee.

"I'm sorry," he said into her hair. "She didn't answer when I called this morning, but I thought she was probably in the shower, so I just left a message. I'm so sorry."

Tash loosened her hold on his neck and slid down to stand on her own feet.

"She's always there, Kevin. Where else could she be?"

"I don't know. Let's look for clues."

Kevin picked up Cap'n Jackie's garage door opener from its hiding place behind a rock and pushed the button. Vanessa's old Volvo crouched alone in the garage. Tash led the way around the car and opened the door to the yard. She pointed at the garden.

"Look how weedy," she said. "Look at the lettuce."

Kevin nodded, taking big strides across the grass and up the wide wooden stairs. He opened the back door. Tash, right behind him, slipped into Cap'n Jackie's shoes.

"Bug?" Kevin pointed at the broken glass on the floor. "Was it like this when you got here?"

"No," she said. "I broke it. The door was locked."

"Locked?"

Tash nodded, watching Kevin's face carefully. Not mad about the broken glass. Puzzled, just like her. He took a big step across the glass, and she followed close behind.

"You looked everywhere?" he asked.

"Yes."

"Basement, too?"

"I didn't go all the way down."

Tash followed on Kevin's heels as they did a thorough check of the basement. Around the furnace, behind the boxes of Nathan's stuff, back in the storage room. Everywhere. Nothing.

"And you checked the Captain's Quarters?" he asked.

"Yes. Everywhere."

"Did you look for a note?"

"No. I didn't think of that."

Kevin carefully checked all the counters and the shelf and the phone desk. He opened the refrigerator. It was empty, except for ketchup and mayonnaise and some pickles and mustard. He closed the fridge and sank into a kitchen chair. Tash sat across from him.

"Looks from the fridge like she was planning to be gone," he said. "Was her bed made upstairs?"

"Everything shipshape," said Tash.

Kevin walked over and put his finger under the top name on the list taped to the wall above the phone: Nathan.

What would he know? Nathan hadn't been home in ages. He hadn't even come for Mulligan's funeral. Too busy with his job, he'd said. When Tash said he was selfish, Cap'n Jackie said Nathan had worked hard to get that set-design job. *If anyone deserves a good job, it's Nathan,* she said. *"Even Mulligan knows that,"* she said.

Kevin punched the number into his phone and waited. *Voice mail,* he mouthed to Tash.

"Hello, Nathan? Kevin McCorry here. Listen, we just got home last night after being gone for a month. Cap'n Jackie's back door was locked this morning, and there's nobody home."

Tash appreciated that he didn't say anything about the broken window.

"Call me back, okay? We're a bit worried over here. There's no note or anything. Fridge is cleaned out, but the car's still in the garage."

He said his number, then put his phone back in his pocket and looked at Tash.

"Well?" he said.

"Well?"

"Get the broom. We've got a mess to clean up here. If you leave a single sliver of glass on the floor and Cap'n Jackie steps on it, we'll never hear the end of it."

NAAYTHAN

SAYS

Kevin waited while Tash gathered some things for the day. She went with him to the Biscuit Jam, and Kevin went back to work in the kitchen. Tash settled onto a stool at the counter. After eggs over easy and a biscuit, she looked through her autograph book from camp. Just the night before last, she and Gwen had been out way past dark collecting autographs from kids in the other cabins.

How could that have been only two nights ago? Already it felt unreal and far away. The clatter of dishes, the whir of the air conditioner, the hot oven smells, and the smooth counter—this was reality now, but it felt so wrong. This wasn't how home was supposed to be. Home was Kevin, sure, but it was also Cap'n Jackie.

"*We're going to practice every day until my so-called agoraphobia and your so-called autophobia are gone.*"

"*It sounds like I'm scared of cars,*" Tash said.

"*Well, agoraphobia sounds like I'm scared of being gored.*"

"*When we're done, I'll be able to sit in a car all day long.*"

"*And I'll get a toro-toro cape and challenge Ferdinand the Bull.*"

"*Ha ha.*"

"*Ha ha.*"

If she hadn't gone to camp, Tash would be ready to stay alone like any normal almost-sixth-grader by now. But then she wouldn't have met Gwen or gone on that horse overnight and had the most fun she'd ever had in her whole life.

What if Cap'n Jackie really had moved to New York? Or what if something even worse had happened?

Dishes crashed in the kitchen. Forks clinked on plates, punctuating the soft jazz from the speakers in the corners. Finally, the brunch-to-lunch rush ended and tables emptied. Kai the Bus Guy cleared the dirty dishes, and Kevin finally came around the corner, ready to leave.

His phone dinged on the way home, and he pulled over to the curb to answer.

"Hi, Nathan." Tash caught her breath. "Yeah, we . . ." Kevin broke off and listened and listened. He cut his eyes sideways to Tash for a quick second and then looked straight ahead. "When was that? Hm. Uh-huh. Yeah, I'll bet. Yup. Yup, okay. Yes. Tomorrow. Tomorrow when I get off work. Okay, Thursday, then? Right. Okay. Okay, bye."

"Tomorrow what? Thursday what?" Tash asked before Kevin got the phone away from his ear.

"Bug."

Tash pulled her feet up on the seat and put her arms around her knees.

"What?"

Kevin's voice was too soft. And why wouldn't he look at her? Were his eyes shiny?

"Cap'n Jackie took a fall. She broke her hip."

Tash's breath rushed out. Broken hip, okay. They'd fix it like they'd fixed Tash's arm when she fell out of Cap'n Jackie's oak tree. Sure, it hurt. Then it got better. Good as new. She stretched that arm out in front of her. It felt fine now.

"So where is she?" she asked.

"They just moved her to rehab yesterday. She'll be there until she's ready to come home."

"Rehab?"

Tash's dad had gone to a rehab place to stop using drugs. They'd helped him get clean and sober so he could be Tash's dad and stay out of trouble. It had worked for a while.

"Not that kind of rehab," said Kevin. "This kind is for older people who need to get physical therapy. It's rehabilitation from an injury, not from drugs."

"Can't she do that at home?"

"No. A broken hip is a big deal, especially for an older person. She needs nursing care."

"So she's with a bunch of strangers?"

Tash couldn't imagine anything worse for Cap'n Jackie. It would be like locking Tash alone in the house for days and days.

"Nathan says she had a rough go in the hospital. They're hoping she'll do better at rehab."

"We have to go and get her out. Right now."

"It's not that easy, Bug. She needs medical care.

Nathan suggested we give her today to settle in. We'll go after work tomorrow."

"Who cares what Naaythan says? I don't."

"Well, you'd better. Nathan is the one making decisions for her."

"Why can't she make her own decisions?"

Kevin took another big breath. He looked out the windshield again.

"When Nathan found Cap'n Jackie, she was unconscious."

Tash squinted at the dashboard.

"How could Nathan find her from New York?"

"He came to visit."

"When we were gone?"

"Yes, he came a couple of weeks ago. He was here until just a couple of days ago. He had to go back and take care of some things."

"Why didn't he call us?"

"He was going to call me today. He thought we were coming home tonight."

Huh. Figures Nathan would get it wrong. Tash scowled out the window as Kevin put the car in gear and pulled away from the curb.

"Cap'n Jackie's okay, right?" she asked.

"The break wasn't a terrible one. She could make a full recovery."

"So she'll be fine, right?"

"That's what we're hoping," said Kevin. "Nathan says if she'll cooperate, she'll do fine."

Cooperate? Cap'n Jackie was good at many things. Cooperating was not one of them.

When Tash took the compost out after dinner, she looked up to the second floor of Cap'n Jackie's house. Why did Nathan have to close all the windows? It made the house look different. Empty. She trudged back up the stairs, and as she drew closer to the door, she heard Kevin on the phone.

"I think that's a good idea," he said. "Align forces."

Who was he talking to? Tash waited on the landing for him to say something else. He stuck his head around the corner and raised his eyebrows.

"Here she is," he said. "Tash, Nathan wants to talk to you."

Why would he want to talk to her? She backed away, but Kevin took the compost bucket and handed her the phone.

"Hello?"

"Hi, Tasha. This is Nathan."

Duh.

"Tasha? Are you there?"

"Yes." She wanted to tell him it was Tash, not Tasha, but it didn't seem like the right time for that. "I'm here."

"You know Cap'n Jackie broke her hip, right? And that she was unconscious for a little while?"

Nathan spoke slowly, as if Tash were five years old and might not know what *unconscious* meant.

"I know. Kevin told me."

Kevin caught her eye and shook his head slightly. *Watch your tone.*

"Cap'n Jackie was very mad at me when she woke up. She was mad that I took her to the hospital."

Well, of course she was.

"She let me have it pretty good, and then she stopped talking. Do you know what the silent treatment is?"

Nobody could know Cap'n Jackie and not know what the silent treatment was. Why did he have to act like he knew her so much better than Tash did?

"She is giving me the silent treatment. She's giving it to the nurses and doctors, too, and that makes it hard for them to help her. So she might not talk to you when you see her."

"Why me? I didn't take her to the hospital."

Tash hoped Cap'n Jackie hadn't told Nathan about her being a little stinker.

"Well, just in case," said Nathan. "Be patient, okay? We need to remind her how much we love her."

"Okay, sure," said Tash. "Here's Kevin."

She handed the phone back, went to her bedroom, and shut the door. Cap'n Jackie was always saying how special Nathan was, how smart he was. He didn't seem that smart to her. He'd been gone a long time, and now she knew Cap'n Jackie way better than he did. She didn't need anyone telling her how to be with the Captain.

"Bug?" Kevin tapped on the door. "Tash, you okay?"

"Fine."

"Can I come in?"

"Whatever."

Kevin sat next to her on the bed, facing the Captain's Quarters window.

"Nathan's sad, you know. And scared."

"He shouldn't have left her with strangers."

"Those strangers are going to help her, and he'll be

back on Thursday. We need to get on the same team, all of us, and help the Captain. Now's not the time for petty jealousies."

"I'm *not* jealous."

"Well, then stop acting like you are. Nathan is doing his very best. Now it's our turn to do our best. Got it?"

Kevin kissed the top of her head and left the room, turning the light out on his way. The streetlight reflected on the glass of Cap'n Jackie's closed window. Tash turned the other way. Cap'n Jackie would be okay. She had to be.

TWICE

FOR

NO

The next afternoon, Kevin turned Terkel in to a broad driveway. The sign said *White Oaks Extended Care and Rehabilitation Center,* but the trees lining the drive were spindly baby maples.

"Those aren't oaks," said Tash.

"Maybe there's some in back." Kevin pulled Terkel into a parking place. "Since when do you identify trees?"

"Since camp."

They got out of Terkel and Tash followed Kevin up the sloped entry sidewalk. A couple of old people in wheelchairs sat in the shade of the building, looking out over the parking lot. Another wheelchair came out through the sliding glass doors. An old guy in a checked shirt was being pushed by a kid around Tash's age. Two parent-type people came behind.

The kid pushed the chair down the slope. Kevin and Tash stepped out of the way.

"Not so fast, Ryan!" called the dad-type person.

"Fast is fine," said the old guy in the chair. "Wind in my hair, Ryan."

The kid and the old guy picked up speed and left the parent types strolling behind. Would Cap'n Jackie be in a wheelchair? Tash could bring her out for a ride. That would get her talking.

"Hang on a minute." Kevin stopped Tash in front of the building. "I want you to be prepared," he said. "Cap'n Jackie was in the hospital for over a week, and Nathan said she hasn't been eating very well. She probably doesn't feel good, and she might be on medication."

"She'll be fine once she sees us," said Tash. "She was just mad at Nathan."

"You might be right, but I'm just saying—she might be different from what you're used to."

Tash stepped in front of the glass doors, and they

slid open. Just to the left was a lounge area, with chairs clustered around a glass birdcage. The cage was big, taller than Kevin, and busy with color and motion. Tash veered over for a look.

They were little, those birds, and all different colors. Green, red, purple, yellow. One was bright light blue with a black head. The birds flitted between nestie holes and perches, down to the floor to peck at scattered seeds, and up again.

"Back off."

Tash jumped at the voice behind her. A girl with wide-frizzed dark hair and glasses was curled into one of the chairs so neatly that Tash hadn't seen her. The girl glared at Tash from above the edge of a book with — Chinese? — writing on the front.

"Don't get so close to the glass," she said. "It stresses them out."

"Who are you?" asked Tash. "The bird manager?"

The girl smiled with closed lips. She pointed to Kevin.

"Your dad's waving at you."

"He's not my dad," said Tash.

The girl nodded and stuck her nose back in the book. Tash ran to catch up with Kevin. They walked down the hall, past a dining-room area where old people were playing some sort of game around a table. They found the elevator at the end of the hall.

"It smells funny here," Tash said as they stepped in. "All chemical-ish."

"Strong cleaning products," said Kevin.

When the elevator doors slid open, Tash followed close on Kevin's heels. They passed open-doored rooms where old people sat in wheelchairs or lay in bed, watching TV, sleeping, or staring into space.

The hall widened, with a picture window on one side and an enormous fish tank on the other. In the center, two nurses sat behind a big curved counter. Fish of various sizes and colors swam around and around, dodging in and out of the sea plants and fake rocks.

Tash watched them while Kevin talked to a nurse. Then he came up behind her, put an arm around her shoulder, and steered her to the next hallway. They walked almost to the end, and Kevin stopped. The sign on the door said JACQUELINE MOSCATO. The door was slightly ajar. Kevin knocked on it.

"Just a minute!" The voice was not Cap'n Jackie's. A toilet flushed. "Mrs. Moscato, it sounds like you have some visitors!"

Mrs. Moscato?

"Come on in!" the voice called.

Kevin pushed the door open. A round woman with blond hair was right there, blocking Tash's view of the room. Pink Tiggers bounced all over her hospital scrubs. Whoever heard of a pink Tigger?

"Well, isn't this nice?" she said. "We just finished freshening up."

The nurse stepped to the side and—was that—? No. Yes? No. The person in the wheelchair was old. Truly old. Her hair was—well, it looked like it would belong to someone named Mrs. Moscato. And her shirt, yes, that looked like one of Cap'n Jackie's shirts, but it was buttoned all the way up, even the top button. Tash took a step back.

"Cap'n Jackie?" Kevin's voice was gentle as only Kevin's could be. "We just got home Saturday night. Nathan told us we could find you here."

The Mrs. Moscato in the wheelchair did not say anything. She didn't even look up.

"Yes, we had a fall." The nurse stepped closer to Kevin and spoke in a lower voice. "Poor thing's had a rough time of it. But we'll get you better before you know it, won't we?" She raised her voice on the last part again, bright and cheery as if she were talking to a little child.

"They do such a good job at our beauty parlor here," she said to Kevin. "Brightens the ladies' days right up, to have their hair done nice."

Tash couldn't believe Cap'n Jackie didn't say anything. She didn't even look up. Cap'n Jackie *hated* being called a lady. Even worse than she hated being called "Mrs."

"And you, dear, what's your name?"

"Tash. And she's not Mrs. Anybody."

Cap'n Jackie still didn't move.

"Well, then, Miss Moscato, I'll leave you to your guests now." The nurse turned to Kevin. "So nice of you to come and visit. Poor dear. Company will be good medicine."

She bustled out. Tash looked up at Kevin. Was this really Cap'n Jackie? Maybe it was a case of mistaken identity. Like babies getting switched in the hospital.

"Cap'n Jackie?" Kevin knelt by the wheelchair and put his hand on the old woman's arm. "It's us. Kevin and the Kid. We're here. We're back."

The old woman did not move. Cap'n Jackie's silent

treatments were loud and full of things unsaid. This was just . . . empty.

"Kevin," Tash whispered. "Can she hear us?"

"I don't know, my Bug. Cap'n Jackie, can you hear me?"

"Tap once if you can hear us," said Tash.

Cap'n Jackie's hands usually flew around as she talked, pointing and slicing the air and stabbing to make a point, or smacking the table. These were old hands, ropy with blue veins and a yellow bruise on the back of one. They didn't move at all.

Tash walked over to the big window that looked out onto a wide expanse of lawn. There was an oak tree in the center. A stone's throw away, if you threw it hard. Only one. Oak. Not Oaks. Kevin pulled up the one chair in the room, settling close to Cap'n Jackie. He launched into a story about the sheep in New Zealand.

Tash swallowed hard and turned back around. Cap'n Jackie didn't seem to hear a word Kevin was saying. She looked so small and fragile and blank. Just as Tash was thinking she really must be an impostor, the right-hand pointer finger raised ever so slightly, and then dropped. And raised and dropped again.

"Kevin! Did you see that?"

"See what?"

"Twice for no!" Tash pointed at Cap'n Jackie's hands. "She tapped twice for no!"

"No what?"

"I told her to tap once if she could hear us. She tapped twice. That means she can't hear us."

They both stared at Cap'n Jackie's fingers.

"Are you sure?" asked Kevin.

"Yes. I saw it."

"But you know that doesn't make sense, right?"

"Yes, it does. It makes perfect sense. That's just what Cap'n Jackie would do, Kevin! So maybe she can't hear us, but she's in there! It's her!"

"Hm." Kevin studied Cap'n Jackie's face again. "Cap'n Jackie, you wouldn't be messing with us, would you?"

Tash kept her eyes riveted on the Captain's hands.

"Once for yes," she whispered. "Twice for no."

The hands did not move again. Tash made a fist and knocked on the wheelchair arm. *THUD. THUD. tap-ta-tap. THUD. THUD. Tap-ta-tap.* She stared at

Cap'n Jackie's hands, watching for any slight shift. Not a finger. Not a twitch.

"We have to get her out of here," said Tash. "Look what they did to her hair."

"Captain Jackie." Kevin spoke directly to the Captain, moving so his face was in front of hers. "Look. We want to bring you home. We'll do whatever we can, but you have to do the physical therapy. You have to get strong again so we can get you out of here."

"I bet she hates them," said Tash. "I would if they did that to my hair."

"I'll talk to them about the hair. And the Mrs. Moscato business." Kevin got to his feet. "Cap'n Jackie, we're going now, but we'll be back tomorrow. And Nathan will be back on Thursday."

"She can't hear you, Kevin," said Tash. "She said so."

Kevin rolled his eyes the way he always did when Tash and Cap'n Jackie agreed on something that shut him out.

"I want to ask the nurses about the drugs, too," said Kevin. "I think she might be overmedicated."

Sure, that was it. Too much medication. Kevin would fix it, and Cap'n Jackie would get better in a hurry.

"Bye, Captain," said Tash. "See you tomorrow."

THE

BIRD

MANAGER

"How about if you go up by the birds while I talk to the nurse?" said Kevin. "Do you remember how to get there?"

Tash was fine with that. She didn't like the nurses. No wonder Cap'n Jackie wouldn't cooperate. Tash wouldn't, either.

She glanced into the rooms as she headed for the elevator. The people did not look very alive. Like that woman there in the hallway. Her eyes were so, so bleary and blank. They reminded Tash of that movie where aliens sucked out people's souls and left their bodies wandering around empty, nobody home.

Maybe White Oaks had a secret soul-sucking machine. They took people's souls and stashed them in a room, and then the aliens came and bought them for a lot of money. Cap'n Jackie's soul would be worth millions. Trillions, maybe.

Tash got in the elevator. It smelled like bleary eyes scrubbed over with pink Tiggers. That smell alone might make you want to shut up forever. Cap'n Jackie would be fine once they got her out of this place.

From the elevator, Tash passed the empty cafeteria. The bird manager was still reading in the lobby. Tash sat in the other chair, farther away from the birds.

"Is this too close?" she asked.

The girl put her book down.

"The chairs are okay. You just shouldn't walk right up to the glass. It scares them."

"What's that?" Tash pointed at the book.

"*Harry Potter* in Japanese."

"You can read that?"

"Sort of," said the girl. "It's slow going."

"Do you speak Japanese?"

"Sometimes."

Tash studied the girl. She didn't exactly look Japanese, but she didn't not.

"If you're getting ready to ask me 'What are you?' don't," said the girl. "I'm human. My genetics are half Japanese, half Ashkenazi Jew. How about you?"

"Also human. Genetics half Irish, half I don't know."

"Which half?"

"Left half."

Tash pointed to the left side of her face. The girl's mouth stretched into another close-lipped smile.

"I'm Naomi," she said. "My mom is a PT here."

"I'm Tash. What's a PT?"

"Physical therapist. I'm supposed to be at camp this week, but my session got canceled, so I have to hang around here."

"Oh."

The bright-blue bird flew to where a lime-green one with a red head was perched. Red Head flew up to the ceiling, and then dropped to the floor. It was a big cage, but not if you wanted to really stretch your wings and go somewhere.

"They're Gouldian finches," said Naomi. "Native to Australia. My mom says it's good for the patients to have some color and life around, but we don't think it's so good for the birds."

"We should let them out," said Tash.

This time Naomi's smile was big enough to show teeth with braces. She nodded.

"It's locked," she said. "We'd need the key to let them out."

"Who has the key?" asked Tash. "They must open it to feed them, right?"

"Right." Naomi nodded. "And to take dead ones out."

"Dead ones?"

"Well, yeah. Nobody lives forever, right? I mean, same with the people here. Sometimes they have to take out the dead ones."

Tash turned away from the birds and looked out the front window at the parking lot. She wished Kevin would hurry up.

"But probably whoever you're visiting won't die," said Naomi. "Not if they're here in the rehab wing. People in this part mostly get better and go home."

Tash nodded, still looking out the window. Get better and go home. That's what Cap'n Jackie needed to do. Get better and go home.

"So who are you visiting?"

Tash turned. The hallway was still empty, no sign of Kevin.

"My friend. She fell and broke her hip," said Tash.

"Is she the one who won't talk? With short white hair?"

Tash nodded.

"I watched her in therapy this morning. My mom says she'd heal up just fine if she'd get with the program. What's her name?"

"Jacqueline Moscato." Tash lifted her chin and stared Naomi straight in the eyes. "I call her Cap'n Jackie."

"What's she captain of?"

"Everything."

Tash narrowed her eyes, daring Naomi to laugh. Naomi didn't so much as smile. She nodded slowly, then her eyes shifted sideways.

"Here comes your not-dad," she said. "I'll tell my mom about Cap'n Jackie. How she's the captain of everything."

"Thanks," said Tash.

"I'm here every day this week," said Naomi. "Eight to four. Are you coming back?"

"Tomorrow."

Naomi nodded. Tash nodded, then turned and followed Kevin out to the parking lot.

THE

HISTORY

OF

MAGIC

The next morning, silence pressed in on Tash before she even got her eyes open. Kevin was gone to work. Was she alone?

A chair scraped the floor in the kitchen. Okay, good. Margaret was there. Tash lay back on the pillow. Margaret wasn't a babysitter. She was Kevin's friend, just hanging out and minding her own business for a while.

Probably by next week, Cap'n Jackie would be home. Tash would help her out around the house, and by the time school started, Cap'n Jackie would be much better. Maybe even walking with a cane again.

Tapping twice for no—that meant her soul was actually still in there. It was puzzling, though. Tapping twice meant both that she could hear and that she couldn't hear.

Maybe she'd been saying no to the pink-Tigger nurse's talk about the nice hairdo. That nurse reminded Tash of Professor Umbridge, with all of her cheery "Isn't that nice?" and "Let's fix your hair pretty." Why would Nathan leave Cap'n Jackie there with her? What was wrong with him?

Tash finally got up, got dressed, and ate a bowl of cereal. Margaret looked over her glasses to say hello and then went back to tapping on her laptop.

"I'm going next door for a while," Tash said as she put her bowl in the sink.

Margaret raised her eyebrows.

"I think I'll clean up the garden, so it'll be nice when Cap'n Jackie gets back."

"Okay," said Margaret. "I'll be here."

Tash thumped downstairs, scooted through the hedge, and looked over the garden. In addition to the bolting lettuce and weeds, the green beans were out of control. Giant zucchini and cucumbers should have been picked days ago.

Tash started by picking off the rotten grape tomatoes and tossing them into the compost. She ate a few sweet ripe ones and piled the rest to take home. Then she pushed each wire cage deeper into the ground.

Tash stood back and slitted her eyes until they were almost closed. She imagined the Captain up on the porch, jabbing her cane at the weeds.

"Git em!" she'd yell. "Tear those weeds up!"

Cap'n Jackie used to handle the garden herself, but earlier this summer she'd given Tash directions from the porch. Her bad hip had been bothering her more, and she'd been using her cane in the house. Kevin said that Cap'n Jackie needed a new hip, but she wouldn't go get it because then she'd have to be in the hospital and rehab.

Tash hadn't even asked which hip broke. If it was the bad one, maybe they fixed it. Once the Captain healed up, she wouldn't even need the cane. That would be good.

After pulling some weeds, Tash wandered back to the berry bush. She ate some raspberries and imagined herself hiding back in the brambles.

She couldn't remember that four-year-old day at all. How had she even gotten into Cap'n Jackie's yard? There was no passage cut through the hedge back then. She would have to have crawled through the dense leafy brush or slunk around the side of the garage.

The berry bush looked like an awfully prickery place to hide. Tash got down on her hands and knees. From this angle, she could see open places where someone really little could crawl in. It was a great place to watch the adults and see what they were up to. And to eat berries. Tash found a handful close to the ground, plumped up and juicy.

She wandered over to Cap'n Jackie's porch and up the back steps. Kevin had pulled the shade down again so "the whole world wouldn't blow in that broken window." Tash opened the door. The house hollered *empty* so loud, she backed away and sat on the top step.

She wanted to go into Cap'n Jackie's house. She wanted to see if she could do it. And she wanted— what? Something. When she'd been in the house the other day, she'd rushed through, looking for and hoping not to find anything horrible. She hadn't taken time to notice things.

Now she wanted to investigate. It shouldn't be so

scary. It was just Cap'n Jackie's house. Cap'n Jackie loved to be alone in there. She said at first after Vanessa died, it was so quiet and lonely, she could hardly stand it. But then one day she picked up the key and held it tight and squeezed her eyes closed, and everything changed.

Cap'n Jackie felt a big warmth all around her, and with her eyes still closed, she saw a huge shape of wings and shadows and glimmer with a crown of dragonflies. Draphin. Half dragon, half dolphin.

Draphin spoke inside of Cap'n Jackie's head. *"Vanessa sent me,"* Draphin said. *"So you won't be lonely."*

Cap'n Jackie talked about Draphin as if she were as real as Mulligan the cat. Tash could not remember a time without Draphin. Even with the key, Tash had never really and truly seen her—not the way Cap'n Jackie did—but Draphin was as much a part of her childhood as Cap'n Jackie.

One time Tash asked Kevin if Draphin was really, really and truly real. He shrugged and said, Who was he to decide what was real? He said *real* had lots of different meanings, and Draphin was real for Cap'n Jackie and real for Tash, and that was good enough for him. But it wasn't quite good enough for Tash.

Maybe, just maybe if she went inside, Draphin would be there. Maybe she'd tell her how to help the Captain. How to make her decide to cooperate. But Tash would have to go into the house alone, and close her eyes and watch and listen.

If only she had the key. Where was the key, anyway? Maybe it was still on the kitchen floor. It must be somewhere in the house. Tash took a deep breath, steeled herself, and stood up. If Cap'n Jackie could get through day after day stuck with strangers and a pink-Tigger nurse, Tash could spend a few minutes in a house by herself.

"Come on, Tash," she said out loud. "Not Bug, not Kid. TASH. No problem. Let's go."

IN

CAP'N

JACKIE'S

HOUSE

Tash walked through the unlocked, broken-windowed back door and into the quiet kitchen. She dropped to her hands and knees and searched the entire kitchen floor. She found dust in the corners, but no key.

She wandered into the living room, checking windowsills and tabletops. More dust, no key. Tash sat in Cap'n Jackie's storytelling chair, the rocker/recliner. When she was Kid, she used to curl up on the squishy blue couch and close her eyes. Mullie would hop up and purr against her chest, settling in for the story.

Cap'n Jackie would call in Draphin. She'd describe her perfectly, the shimmering scales and indigo eyes, the smooth gray tapering of her fluked tail. Draphin, who could swim through glass, would land in the living room, and they'd all climb on. Mullie would perch on the curve of Draphin's neck. The Captain stood between the mighty wings, and the Kid flipped along behind on the flukes. Draphin flew them out the window and into other worlds.

Back in the napping days, Tash would fall asleep midstory, and the stories and her dreams mixed together until it was hard to tell which was which. Tash pushed the recliner back and stretched out with her eyes closed. She fisted her hand, trying to feel the key in it.

"Are you there, Draphin?" she whispered.

She waited, listening hard. Instead of Draphin, the emptiness of the house crept up her sides and circled cold hands around her throat. Tash shuddered and sat up straight, eyes wide open. She banged the recliner back into rocking chair mode and stood up.

Okay, she was okay. *Breathe in, breathe out, like Kevin says. Stomp your feet on the floor. Look at what's real in the room.*

On the living-room wall opposite the recliner, a

framed Vanessa and Cap'n Jackie waltzed across a dance floor. Cap'n Jackie wore a tuxedo, and her short hair was dark without any sign of gray. Vanessa was elegant in a long, flowing dress. She wasn't as tall as the Captain, but her high-wrapped hair made her look taller.

"Vanessa always loved a waltz. She'd close her eyes, and I'd spin her around the dance floor, smooth as a Draphin flight."

Vanessa was the Captain's, just like Nathan. Once, a long time ago, Tash put her secret fear into words.

"I think you like Nathan better than me."

"Why would you say that?"

"Well, he looks like Vanessa and I don't. And you love Vanessa best."

"If you want to get into looks, Mulligan is the most beautiful of all."

Cap'n Jackie hadn't denied it, and Tash never forgot. She picked up the framed picture of Mullie on the coffee table. Back in May, Kevin had helped her pick out the frame and gift wrap it for Cap'n Jackie's birthday. Nathan hadn't even come back for Mullie's funeral.

"If Naaaythan's so great, where is he?"

"Don't you take that tone about Nathan. He's had to deal with things you can't even dream of."

Well, he'd never had to deal with any of this. He'd had Cap'n Jackie right there with him all the time, and Vanessa and Mulligan, too. The silence pressed in and squeezed Tash's chest. She put the picture down.

Maybe Cap'n Jackie had left the key on her night-stand like Tash did. Tash opened the door to the Captain's Quarters and looked up. She could easily imagine Cap'n Jackie standing at the top. But in her mind, Cap'n Jackie did not fall. She threw the cane down and dove, reaching for Draphin's tail.

But that's not what happened. Cap'n Jackie fell. She fell and landed on the floor.

Tash stepped back. Right there. She probably landed right there.

Kevin said that Cap'n Jackie had lain there for a day and a half, unable to move. If it had been Tash, she would have died just from the weight of *alone* standing on her ribs, crushing them and breaking them and poking them into her lungs and all the air would rush out and they'd stab her heart until it spilled out all over the floor and she'd be dead.

But not Cap'n Jackie. No. Cap'n Jackie was never afraid to be alone. She was much more afraid of a crowd. And now she was trapped in a crowd of strangers. Tash turned and sat on the bottom step and dropped her head into her hands. She rubbed her eyes, looking down at the floor. And in the corner of the doorway, tucked under the lip of the bottom step—there it was!

Tash snatched the key from the floor. She laid it on her palm and squeezed her fingers tight over the top like she'd done thousands of times over the last few years. She could almost feel Cap'n Jackie's hand curled around hers, could almost hear her voice.

"This is it, right here. This key unlocks doors in your mind to imagination and flight. With this key, no matter what happens, you're always free."

Tash stroked the key with the tip of one finger. It must have flown down the stairs with Cap'n Jackie. She probably squeezed it in her fist while she lay here alone for hours and hours.

Why hadn't Nathan taken it along to the hospital? It was his own aunt's key—he must know what it meant to Cap'n Jackie. Tash closed her eyes and squeezed it tight. The familiar shape indented the skin of her palm. She searched the darkness behind her lids for some sign of Draphin. Instead, she saw Cap'n Jackie's eyes the night she'd thrown the key. The way they'd widened in surprise. And then hurt, as if Tash had punched her in the nose.

Tash popped her eyes open and looked down at the key resting on her palm. She had been so wrong to throw it. Cap'n Jackie was trapped at White Oaks. Tash would give her the key and set her free.

FIGHTING

WORDS

Tash pulled the back door closed behind her. Margaret looked up and nodded, but didn't say anything. Tash twirled the key around and around her fingers. Nearly two hours until Kevin would be home.

Margaret tapped away on her laptop at the kitchen table. Tash made herself a peanut butter sandwich and took it to the living room. She pulled *My Neighbor Totoro* from the DVD pile and turned on the TV. Cap'n Jackie loved that movie, even more than Tash did.

"Now that—that's a movie! That's how movies ought to be."

Most of all, Cap'n Jackie loved the grinning cat bus.

"See? I'm not the only one who's crazy. Someone made up a flying cat bus. That's crazier than anything I ever came up with."

Tash didn't love the movie quite as much as Cap'n Jackie did, but she liked it well enough to watch it all the way through, twirling the key through her fingers. Kevin came home just as the final credits were playing, and Tash slipped the key into her pocket. Kevin probably wouldn't like it that she'd been prowling around the Captain's house by herself. Nobody had told her not to, but it was probably better not to mention it.

"Get your shoes," said Kevin. "Let's go see the Captain."

Tash couldn't wait to show Cap'n Jackie the key. She and Kevin blew past the lobby, which was empty except for the birds. They took the elevator to the lower level, and Tash followed Kevin down the long corridor and past the nurse's station.

When they turned into Cap'n Jackie's room, it was empty. Nobody in the bed. No wheelchair.

"Kevin?" Tash grabbed Kevin's arm. "Where is she?"

"I don't know, Bug," he said. "Let's check the nurse's station."

The nurse at the desk told them that "Mrs. Moscato" was in physical therapy.

"Ms. Moscato," Kevin corrected, although that wasn't much better.

"It's nobody's business if I'm married, and I'm not a mzzzz, either. Call me Captain."

"They'll bring her back to her room before long," said the nurse. "You're welcome to wait for her there."

Back in Cap'n Jackie's room, Kevin sat in the only chair. Tash paced around the room, stopping to look out the big picture window.

"I don't see why they call it White Oaks," she said. "They should call it Puny Little Maples, or Red Oak. That's a red oak out there."

"You learned all that at camp?" asked Kevin.

"Yup."

"I guess camp turned out not to be so bad," he said.

"Yup."

"Who was right?"

Tash rolled her eyes.

"Come on, say it," said Kevin. "Who was right?"

"If I hadn't gone to camp, Cap'n Jackie wouldn't be trapped here now."

"Oh, no," said Kevin. "You can't go down that road, Bug."

"I'm not Bug."

"Well, Tash can't go down it, either. We do what we do; we make the best choices we can. She might have fallen even if you had been there."

"Yeah, but she wouldn't have been lying there alone for two days."

"That's a fact," said Kevin. "But still. You can't make this your fault. Or mine, in case you were headed that way."

"Then whose fault is it? Cap'n Jackie's?"

"There's not always a fault, you know. Sometimes things happen."

Tash pressed her nose to the glass. The yard stretched out big and wide. One squirrel chased another across the grass and up the trunk of the red oak.

"How long till Cap'n Jackie comes back?" she asked the window.

"You heard the nurse. Before long."

"But what does that mean, exactly?" She turned to look at Kevin. "How much before long? Because it already seems kind of long."

96

"I don't know, Tash. It might be a while."

"Can I go up and look at the birds?"

"Sure." Kevin slouched back in the chair and pulled his phone out of his pocket. "Come back before long."

"How long before long?"

"Ha." Kevin dove into his phone and waved her away without looking. "Go."

Tash hurried by the nurses and the fish. She pressed the up button and waited for the elevator.

"Hi."

Tash whirled. Naomi was right behind her.

"Where's your not-dad?" she asked.

"Kevin's in Cap'n Jackie's room." Tash pointed over her shoulder. "Cap'n Jackie's in physical therapy—with your mom?"

"No." Naomi shook her head. "I just came from there. She's in OT now."

"What's that?"

"Occupational therapy. They practice dressing and cooking and stuff—activities of daily living, they call it—so they can get along at home. But Cap'n Jackie's not doing anything. She's just sitting there, and the OT is on her phone."

The elevator doors opened, but Tash hesitated.

"Maybe I should go tell Kevin."

"It won't do any good. If anyone comes in, Marcia—that's the OT—will suddenly start doing stuff. My mom says Marcia is so lazy it's criminal, but she's smart so she never gets caught."

Naomi pushed the button, and the elevator took them up to the main floor.

"I was watching Cap'n Jackie in PT this morning." Tash and Naomi passed the cafeteria and the front desk. "She's slick. She acts like she can't see or hear anything, but I caught her looking at me out of the corner of her eye."

Why would Cap'n Jackie look at Naomi and not look at her very own Kid? Maybe she didn't really look. Maybe Naomi just thought she had. Tash stopped a few feet back from the birds with her arms crossed.

"What grade are you going into?" asked Naomi.

"Sixth."

"Me too. What school?"

"Riverside."

"Hey, me too!" said Naomi. "I don't know anyone else going there. I got homeschooled until now."

"Lucky," said Tash.

Cap'n Jackie had talked about homeschooling Tash back in third grade. Tash got her hopes all up until Kevin researched and found out how much stuff you had to do to prove it was really school and not just staying home all day. He and Cap'n Jackie agreed Tash should keep going to regular school.

"Yup," said Naomi. "Except my dad and I were starting to drive each other crazy. Plus he got a different job last spring, and now he has to go into the office every day. So, you probably have a whole pile of friends going to Riverside." She said it with half of a question mark on the end.

"Not exactly."

The birds were all different colors, green and red and yellow. Only one was blue. Bright light blue. That one was Tash's favorite, all by itself on the swing up in the corner.

"Hey, Tash." Naomi's voice was quiet.

Tash turned to look at her.

"My mom's kinda worried about Cap'n Jackie."

"Why?"

"People who break a hip, they have to move. They have to get better or they keep getting worse."

"Worse how?"

"Weaker. More sick. My mom's afraid Cap'n Jackie has decided to just quit."

"Cap'n Jackie's no quitter," Tash snapped.

Naomi's eyes widened. Gwen would have snarled right back, but Naomi wasn't Gwen. She wasn't a snarler.

"I'm sorry," said Tash. "It's just . . . I'd better get back down there."

GOOD

FRIENDS

Tash hurried back through the halls. The whole place made her snarly, with all of the fake-happy decorations. Everything looked like a pink Tigger. Now Naomi probably wouldn't like Tash. Most people didn't like snarlers unless they were one. Well, except for Kevin.

The door to Cap'n Jackie's room was open. Kevin had pulled the chair up next to the bed. Cap'n Jackie was lying there with her eyes closed.

"Is she sleeping?" Tash whispered.

"I don't think so." Kevin spoke in a normal voice. "She just came back a few minutes ago. They said occupational therapy tired her out."

Liars, thought Tash.

She looked around. The only place to sit was the empty wheelchair, so she sat in it and crossed her arms.

"Kevin, what happens if Cap'n Jackie gets worse instead of better?"

Kevin twisted his mouth sideways. His shoulders went up and down with a big breath.

"There's no reason she can't get better," he said. "I talked about it with Nathan last night. The break wasn't a bad one—the surgery repaired it. Unfortunately it was her good hip, not the bad one. But still. If she'll do the therapy and work at it, she should be able to go home and live independently again."

"Do you think the hip hurts her a lot?"

"It's hard to tell," said Kevin. "She's on a fair amount of pain medication, although they've tapered it down some."

Tash leaned forward. Cap'n Jackie's face didn't move at all, but Tash didn't think she was sleeping. She looked more like she was faking.

"Quitter," said Tash.

"Bug!" Kevin said. "Don't say that."

"Well, if she is," said Tash. "I mean, she's acting like one, right?"

"We have no idea what any of this is like for her."

"Cap'n Jackie, are you a quitter?"

Nothing moved. Not Cap'n Jackie's face. Not her fingers. Nothing. Tash sat back in the wheelchair and crossed her arms again.

"If she could hear me, that would've made her mad. Nobody likes a quitter—she says that all the time."

"I don't think she's a quitter," said Kevin. "I think she has her own agenda."

"What's that mean?"

"It means, when can you ever make Cap'n Jackie do anything?"

But Tash had just the thing to make her want to do something.

"Kevin? Can I have some privacy with Cap'n Jackie?"

"Sure. I'll wait out by the fish tank."

He left, and Tash scooted in closer. She put her hand out to touch Cap'n Jackie's hand but then stopped. What if—she imagined Cap'n Jackie sitting up like the dead bathtub lady in the movie. Growling like a zombie, or laughing at her. No, no, this is *Cap'n Jackie*. She wouldn't do that, even if she was dead. Would she?

"Cap'n Jackie?" Tash said. "Hey, I found the key."

No reaction.

"Do you want it back now?"

Tash pulled it out of her pocket and held it up.

"See? It's right here. Open your eyes."

The sheets moved up and down just slightly with Cap'n Jackie's breathing.

"I went to your house today while Kevin was at work, and I found this at the bottom of the stairs. Maybe you dropped it when you fell?"

Tash turned the key over and over in her fingers.

"You got my letter, right? Where I said I was sorry?"

Did Cap'n Jackie's eyes move under the lids? Maybe just a little.

"Did you get it? Tap once for yes."

Cap'n Jackie's hands didn't move. Not one finger.

"I don't know if you can hear me," said Tash. "Are you asleep, or pretending?"

Still nothing.

"You said in your letters that you weren't mad anymore. You're not, right?"

Someone knocked softly, and the door swung all the way open. Tash slipped the key back in her pocket. She couldn't just leave it lying there. One of the nurses might take it.

"Hello there." This nurse was tall and thin, with glasses, and blue and purple flowers on her scrubs. No Tiggers. "How's our patient doing?"

"Fine," said Tash.

She didn't trust any of these nurses.

"Well, it's good you're here. We'll all just keep talking to her, and one of these days, somebody will say something she wants to answer."

This nurse came around to the other side of the bed and picked up Cap'n Jackie's hand, feeling her pulse. Tash leaned back. It sure was hard to get any privacy around here.

"Tash?" Kevin was in the doorway. "Come on, let's let the Captain get some rest."

"The captain?" The nurse looked up with a smile.

"Yes, we call her Cap'n Jackie," said Kevin.

"Cap'n Jackie it is, then." The nurse looked back

down with a smile. "You've got some good friends here, Cap'n Jackie."

Tash needed to see Cap'n Jackie without Kevin or the nurses hanging around. Next time she wouldn't waste it talking. She'd put the key in Cap'n Jackie's palm. Once Cap'n Jackie felt the key in her hand, she'd hold it tight and squeeze her eyes closed, and everything would change. She'd see Draphin and feel better, and then she'd do the PT and come home.

"We'll be back tomorrow, Captain," said Kevin. "Come on, Tash."

Tash had to get into the room alone, and for longer than just a few minutes. But how?

A

DARING

PLAN

Tash had an idea on the way up in the elevator. She'd
need Naomi to make it work. She was relieved to see
Naomi's sneaker dangling over the armchair in front
of the birds.

"Just a sec," she said to Kevin. "I have to talk to the
bird manager."

Tash hustled over to the chair and dropped to one
knee so she could whisper without Kevin hearing.

"Are you mad?" she asked.

"At what?" Naomi looked over her book.

"Me."

"Nope."

Tash looked carefully to see if she was lying.

"Nope." Naomi said it again, looking right back at her. "You said you were sorry."

"Okay, good. Will you be here tomorrow?"

"Yes," Naomi answered. "Why are we whispering?"

Tash put her finger to her lips. Then, keeping her body as a shield, she pointed her thumb back toward Kevin.

"I'm coming by myself," she whispered.

"What time?"

"Um. I don't know exactly. Morning. Like nine, maybe?"

"I'll be here."

Naomi whispered from the side of her mouth and didn't nod or even glance over her shoulder. Tash walked back over to Kevin.

"Does the bird manager have a name?" he asked.

"It's Naomi."

"Bye, Naomi," he called.

A hand popped up over the back of the chair and waved. Kevin being Kevin, he didn't ask any other questions. He didn't say anything for a while. That was good, because it gave Tash a chance to pay attention to where they were going.

Right turn out the drive. Four blocks. Then a left on Lake Street. She knew Lake Street. They were on the other side of town, but she was pretty sure the 21 bus ran from their neighborhood all the way across.

"Anything you want to talk about?" Kevin asked.

"Nope."

"How did it go with Margaret this morning?"

"Fine."

A bus was coming toward them. Yes. The 21. Good.

"Tash, we'll figure things out with the Captain. Nathan's been researching some options. When he gets here on Thursday, we'll all put our heads together."

Tash didn't need Nathan's head or his research. She had her own plan.

"I'm okay, Kevin," she said. "I mean, maybe I'm ready to try staying alone. Maybe I could try it tomorrow, just to see how it goes."

"Are you sure?" he asked.

"You have short shift tomorrow, right?"

"Yes. I'll be home around noon."

"So that's almost nothing, right? If I get lonely, I'll

go to Cap'n Jackie's yard and pull weeds. I'll pretend she's inside doing the dishes or something."

Lonely. That was code. Kevin understood about "lonely" better than anybody, better than Tash even. She wouldn't even know why she got "lonely" if Kevin hadn't told her. When she searched back in her memory, back to living with her daddy, all she had was a fuzzy picture of the biggest and strongest and best person in the whole world. She remembered swinging high at the park one time, high as the green trees, and laughing. She remembered riding on her daddy's shoulders and putting her fingers into his thick dark brown hair.

Kevin said Daddy had a disease that made him forget he wasn't supposed to drink alcohol. One time he did, and went out with some friends and left Tash asleep in their apartment. They got arrested. Kevin said drinking and drugs could make you forget everything important, like that you had a little kid who was home all alone. She was there for two whole days before Grandfather McCorry came and found her hiding in the closet.

Even though Tash couldn't remember that at all, the scared feeling had a life of its own. It crept in when she was alone in a house, wrapped its cold, long-ago fingers around her, and held her frozen at three years old.

But Tash wasn't three. That was a long time ago, and it made no sense to be scared, because Kevin didn't do anything illegal ever, not ever. He didn't even drink beer or wine or anything. He always came home when he said he would. Always. The whole time she'd lived with him.

She'd have to bust through "lonely" to make her plan work. If Cap'n Jackie could get through day after day with all those strangers around her, surely Tash could handle one morning.

"Maybe I won't get so lonely," she told Kevin. "I'm older now. Like you said. I grew up at camp some."

"Tell you what," Kevin said. "I'll tell Margaret you're flying solo, and I'll leave my cell phone on your nightstand. If you wake up and feel lonely, call Margaret, and she'll come over right away. Or call me at work. Okay?"

"Okay."

He was her Kevin, and he was good. She felt bad about lying to him. Not because she'd get in trouble but because she didn't want him to think she was getting to be like her dad. Unreliable and impulsive, that's what Grandfather McCorry said about Daddy. A liar from the moment he could talk. Can't do the right thing to save his life, never could.

Tash wasn't like that. She'd never be like that. This wasn't really a lie. She just wasn't telling Kevin everything.

EXECUTION

Tash woke to silence and looked at the clock: 7:59. Excellent. She had plenty of time. Last night she had Google-mapped on Kevin's laptop when he wasn't looking and checked the route. Walk three blocks to Lake Street, cross at the light, get on the 21. Ride for twenty-five minutes, get off, turn right, walk four blocks, turn left into the driveway. She could do that.

The night before, Tash talked Kevin into a game of Parcheesi that slid past her usual bedtime. Then she made herself stay awake as long as she could, listening to the murmur of Kevin's voice on the phone. Better not to wake up early to an empty house. The sun was well up, and Tash was . . .

Alone. Alone, alone, alone. The apartment buzzed with it. Tash sat up before it could settle on her skin. She was dressed and out the door by 8:10 with the key and Kevin's phone in one pocket and a bunch of quarters in the other.

Alone was not bad when you were going somewhere. People popped out front doors with briefcases and backpacks. Three joggers passed, and four dog-walkers. Tash stopped to pet Tazz, her favorite yellow Lab puppy from the next block over. Golden sunshine rays stretched through the leafy treetops. Tash sniffed. The air smelled like back-to-school time.

She pulled Kevin's phone out of her pocket and put it on Do Not Disturb. She didn't need it going off while she was sneaking around White Oaks. If Kevin called, she could call him back later and say she'd been in the bathroom or something. He'd never even know she'd been gone. Cap'n Jackie wouldn't tell on her, even if she was talking. Which maybe by this afternoon she would be.

Tash reached Lake Street and crossed at the light. Several other people waited at the bus stop. Tash had ridden the 21 with Kevin a number of times, but she'd never ridden it on her own. When the bus approached, she lined up behind a woman with two toddlers.

She got on the bus and dropped her quarters in and sat next to a teenage girl with earbuds. That was the easy part. Getting off at the right place for White Oaks might be harder. The girl with the earbuds got off by the high school and Tash slid over next to the window, keeping a close eye out for landmarks. She had to get off by a McDonald's. No, not that one. Another one.

The bus moved along Lake Street, picking people up and dropping them off. A couple of women with babies in strollers spoke in Spanish. The tall guy across the aisle bobbed his head, moving his lips.

Taking the bus by herself to see Cap'n Jackie was a very grown-up thing to do. She really, truly was not a child anymore. Not a Bug and not a Kid and not a Tasha. She was Tash, and she could do this.

She reached into her pocket and wrapped her hand around the key. Speaking or no speaking, nurse or no nurse, Tash would make sure the key was in Cap'n Jackie's hand before she left White Oaks this morning. The Captain believed in the magic much more than Tash did, so it would work on her. She had to get better. She just had to—that's all.

Tash looked out, saw the McDonald's, and yanked the cord. The bus went another block to the bus stop, and she got off. She walked back to the McDonald's. Yes, this was the street. She turned left.

She was in a part of the city she'd never walked through before, and it was different being on foot. She was right in the middle of things. Teenage boys played soccer in the park. A group of toddlers holding hands in a chain came along the sidewalk, with an adult on each end. Tash skirted the chain of tiny people, feeling very tall.

Farther down the block, a big black dog startled her with a deep bark. Tash leaped sideways, almost falling off the curb. The dog wagged its tail and followed her to the corner of the yard, still barking.

Tash stopped to check the map on the phone, finding the blue dot that was her. Yes, she was only two blocks from White Oaks Rehabilitation Center. By the end of the first block, she recognized the driveway ahead. A skippy feeling danced between her heart and stomach. Something giddy and alive, happy and nervous and a little bit proud.

She'd done it. She'd gotten up and out of the apartment and onto the bus and off the bus and all the way here. If she could do this, surely she could get herself up and ready for school in the morning (*every* morning?) alone. She'd just stop in at Cap'n Jackie's for breakfast like any normal person.

Tash crossed the parking lot and entered through the sliding glass doors. Naomi was there waiting, just like she'd said she would be.

"You're early." Naomi stood to greet Tash. "It's not even nine. How'd you get here?"

"Bus."

"By yourself?"

"Yup. Kevin's at work." Tash glanced at the woman at the front desk, who was looking their way. "Is there someplace outside we can talk?"

Naomi dropped her book on the chair and they headed out the front doors. When they got outside, Naomi hooked a sharp right around the building. The sidewalk sloped gradually down and ended at a low brick wall. Naomi sat on top of it, and Tash sat, too, her legs dangling. The back lawn was about a three-foot drop below.

"That Cassandra at the front desk is a big snoop-nose," said Naomi. "She thinks she's my babysitter or something."

"Will we get in trouble?" asked Tash. "Is it okay for kids to come here without an adult?"

"I don't know. I've never seen anyone do it. Do you ride around on the bus a lot?"

"Yup, we take the bus lots of places."

"I've never even been on a bus." Naomi looked at her the way Tash had looked at Gwen when she'd found out Gwen stayed alone after school every day. "I mean, I've been on the camp bus. But not the kind where you ride around the city."

"It was my first time doing it alone," Tash admitted. "It was easy."

"So what's the plan?"

"I have something I want to give Cap'n Jackie. It's kind of secret. Do you think I can just walk in there? Will anyone stop me?"

"She's in PT now," said Naomi. "She's in the early group; I checked. When do you have to leave by?"

118

"Eleven. What time will she get done?"

"Depends on the day. I can do some recon and find out." Naomi jumped to her feet. "You stay here. Nobody will see you. I'll be back in, like, ten minutes."

Naomi left, and Tash leaned back against the building. The brick wall sloped gradually down to meet the rising hill of the White Oaks backyard. After a few minutes of waiting, Tash got fidgety. She walked along the top of the wall to the end. A row of balconies stretched out above her, and window after window lined up below. A couple of old people sat out on the second-floor balconies, but nobody even looked Tash's way.

She put her hands in her pockets and strolled out into the wide expanse of yard, circling away from the building. She tried to figure out which of those windows was Cap'n Jackie's. She wished she could just swim through glass like Draphin. She'd hide in the room and wait till there were no nurses hanging around and then pop out and surprise the Captain.

A whistle shrilled Tash's attention back to the wall. Naomi was there, waving at her. Tash started to run, then stopped. She put her hands in her pockets and made herself walk slowly, just in case someone was watching.

"So?" she asked. "What'd you find out?"

"Cap'n Jackie's back in her room, but the halls are really busy right now with nurses and meds and stuff. It'll settle down in a half hour or so."

"Do those windows open?"

"No. You can't talk to her from out here."

"That's okay. I just want her to see I'm here so she's ready for me. Then I'll sneak in when the hall's more clear."

Naomi popped up and walked the wall the same way Tash had earlier.

"See the oak?" Naomi pointed. "Let's do recon from there."

The two of them walked over to the big oak centered on the back lawn, doing their best to look casual. Then they tucked in behind the trunk where nobody could see them.

"I love this tree." Naomi petted the bark. "I think it's funny that it gets credit for being plural."

"I noticed that," said Tash. "And it's a red oak, not white."

"How do you know?"

"The leaves." Tash stood to pull a leaf down close. "See? The leaves are pointy. On a white oak, they're rounded."

"So to be accurate, they should've called this place Red Oak."

"That's what I told Kevin," said Tash. "Or Spindly Little Maples, after the trees along the driveway."

"Or Caged Gouldian Finches. Caged Gouldian Finches at the End of Spindly Little Maple Road."

"That's way too long to get on a sign."

"You're right," said Naomi. "We'd make better spies than advertisers."

The sun was warm, the grass still sparkled with dew, and the tree made a nice backrest. If things were different, she'd want to stay and hang out with Naomi—but she had business to tend to.

"Do you think anyone will notice me walking up to Cap'n Jackie's window?"

"You have to be careful. If they think you're a Peeping Tom, there'll be a big fuss. That happened to me last year. I wasn't peeping, I was just walking along looking at a squirrel, but this one lady went ballistic, and then I couldn't be here the rest of the summer. So you need to know exactly where you're going."

"I think it's that one. Third from the end."

Tash pointed to the far end of the building.

"No." Naomi shook her head. "I checked. She's in one thirty-four and it goes up to one forty on that end. So . . . it's that one. Fourth from the end."

Tash leaned around the tree trunk to look.

"Be careful, okay?" said Naomi. "If you get in trouble, I have to ditch you and run for it. My mom will kill me if I get caught at something like this again."

"Okay." Tash didn't want to get ditched, but that was fair. "If I get caught, I won't tell anyone you helped me. I'll pretend I don't even know you."

"Thanks."

Tash left Naomi at the tree and circled wide, close to the bushes on the edge of the property. Then she cut in, sidling up to the corner of the building. Naomi leaned from behind the tree to give her a thumbs-up. Tash walked fast past the first three windows and stopped just before Cap'n Jackie's window with her back tight against the brick wall. She leaned over to peek in the window. All she could see was drapes, so she edged a bit closer.

Cap'n Jackie's foot was right next to the window. Tash recognized her blue-and-gold sneaker. Tash took a deep breath and stepped out in the open. She and the Captain were very close, only the glass between them. Cap'n Jackie met Tash eyeball to eyeball for a flash of a second and Tash saw her in there — saw her eyes widen and light up. And just as fast, the connection was gone. Cap'n Jackie's head dropped before Tash could get the key out of her pocket.

Tash tapped the key on the glass. Cap'n Jackie didn't look up. Tash clicked the key on the glass more deliberately. *TAP. TAP. Tip-ta-tic. TAP. TAP. Tip-ta-tic.* Cap'n Jackie's head didn't move but — wait. What was that?

The pointer finger on the Captain's right hand lifted and dropped. Once. Twice. Twice for no.

WHAT'S

IT

MEAN?

No . . . what? That didn't even make sense. Tash tapped again with the key. Cap'n Jackie did not move. She slumped in the wheelchair as if she never had moved and never would.

Tash gently hit the glass with the side of her fist, then tapped with her knuckles.

THUD. THUD. Tap-ta-tap.

Naomi whistled, and Tash looked out to the oak. A hand snaked around the trunk and waved Tash away from the window. Tash spun back and flattened herself against the brick. She waited, watching Naomi's hand and breathing hard.

And wondering. Cap'n Jackie had seen her for sure. It was the only time they had met eyes since Tash got home. So the twice was definitely no, definitely a message to her. Maybe it was a big no to everything that was happening? Or it might be code for something else. Something that starts with *N*? Naomi? Was Cap'n Jackie trying to say something about Naomi?

Naomi's hand snuck out from behind the oak trunk again and crooked a finger, signaling Tash back to the tree. Tash longed to sneak one more peek to see what was happening in Cap'n Jackie's room. She turned toward the window and glanced over at the oak. The hand frantically waved her away from the window.

Tash ran past the three end windows to the edge of the lawn and made a wide circle back to the tree. She and Naomi both slid down with their backs to the trunk, hidden from view.

"What happened?" Tash asked.

"Lisa the nurse came in. I don't think she saw you, but she saw something. She came right up to the window and looked for the longest time. It's good you didn't stick your face back in there."

"What did Cap'n Jackie do?"

"Nothing. She just sat there."

Tash looked down at her own hands and swallowed hard.

"Naomi, is this an evil place?"

"My mom wouldn't work at an evil place," Naomi said. "But people don't like being here. They all want to go home. My mom helps them meet their goals and get better so they can."

"What happens if they don't meet their goals? Like, if they won't cooperate?"

"Some of them get moved to the south wing," said Naomi. "They never go home again."

Tash could not let that happen. Cap'n Jackie was trapped behind glass, just like the little birds. She couldn't feel the blue-sky breeze or smell the grass or put her hands in the dirt.

"Can they make her stay if she wants to leave?" asked Tash. "Or if her family says they'll take care of her at home?"

"There's these meetings called care conferences," said Naomi. "They decide who goes home when. My mom does those meetings all day on Thursdays."

Tash checked her watch: 10:15. She didn't have much more time. If Cap'n Jackie was going to swim through the glass, she needed the key. She needed it in her hand where she could squeeze it and see the magic.

"I'm going in," said Tash. "You think they'll try and stop me?"

"Just walk in like you know what you're doing. They might not even notice you."

They agreed that they should go back in separately. Naomi would go first and sit by the birds. Tash would swing through a few minutes later and head straight to Cap'n Jackie's room.

"Put on your invisibility cloak," said Naomi. "Low profile."

Tash waited until Naomi had time to get settled. Then she walked through the sliding glass doors and headed straight down the hall. Nosy Cassandra didn't even look up. Past the chatter and clank of the cafeteria, around the corner to the elevator. When the doors opened, Tash moved aside to let two old women with walkers pass. She slipped into the elevator and pressed G for the ground floor.

The patient rooms were mostly empty, but the hall was cluttered with carts carrying food trays and cleaning supplies. Tash passed on silent feet, appreciating the high counter at the nurse's station. She was tempted to drop to her hands and knees and crawl past but decided that might be overkill.

As she headed down the hallway, she heard *hoo hoo hoo*. Like a—pigeon? Or a baby owl? The sound grew louder as she walked, and then suddenly stopped. Tash looked in the rooms she passed, searching for the bird. As she checked a room on the left, she almost ran into the pedals of a wheelchair parked in a doorway on the right. She caught her balance and looked into the pale, empty eyes of the man in the chair. His chalky lips formed a circle. *Hoo-hoo. Hoo-hoo.*

Tash jumped back, her heart double-skipping. She trotted the rest of the way to Cap'n Jackie's room. The door was open and—yes!—nobody was in there but the Captain. Tash started to close the door behind her but realized that would look suspicious.

"Hi, Cap'n Jackie," she said.

The Captain still faced the window. She didn't turn her head or move at all.

"I said hi. It's me, Tash."

She walked over to stand next to the wheelchair.

"Did you see my friend Naomi out there? She's been helping me. Her mom is your physical therapist."

Still nothing.

"I brought the key. We're going to get you out of here."

Tash knelt by the wheelchair and turned over one of Cap'n Jackie's hands. It was completely limp, as if nobody lived inside that skin. Tash pressed the key into Cap'n Jackie's palm. Her fingers didn't close, and the key slid out onto her lap.

"Cap'n Jackie," Tash whispered sharply. "What's wrong?"

She put her nose right up next to Cap'n Jackie's. The Captain closed her eyes.

"No—what?" Tash hissed in a whisper. "You said no. I *saw* it. I saw you tap twice for no. What's it mean?"

Cap'n Jackie's breath wasn't quite steady. Tash placed a finger just below her eyebrow and tried to open the eye. The lid stayed down.

Tash wanted to yell. She wanted to throw something. She put all of her yelling-throwing into a teeth-gritted whisper.

"Cap-tin Jack-EE."

She picked the key up and set it in Cap'n Jackie's limp palm again. This time, she curled the Captain's fingers down and circled her own hands around the fist and the key, the way Cap'n Jackie had done with her all those years ago.

"Come on, do it like you did before," said Tash. "After Vanessa died. Make the magic work. Make Draphin come."

She stepped back, arms crossed. She squeezed her hands tight in her armpits so she wouldn't reach out and shake Cap'n Jackie to wake her up. She should be awake. She should care. She should care about Tash.

Tash couldn't pitch a rager. Not here. Frustration built, rising in her chest, heating her neck and face. She'd never stood still for rage like this before. She could hardly even breathe.

Then, just as Tash's head was about to burst into flames, Cap'n Jackie moved. She lifted her hand, moved it out beyond the arm of the wheelchair, and opened her fingers. The key dropped to the floor with a clink and lay there. Cap'n Jackie's hand returned to her lap.

"Well, look who's back!" The pink-Tigger nurse startled Tash. This time, she was decorated with My Little Ponies. "Where's your daddy, dear?"

Tash put her foot on the key.

"He's not my daddy."

"Well, really, dear, we shouldn't be in here by ourselves."

"I'm not by myself. I'm with her."

Tash pointed at Cap'n Jackie, who sat there like a lump of a bump of nothing.

"Oh, dear."

The nurse turned and hurried out of the room. Tash knelt and grabbed the key.

"I gotta run." Tash grabbed Cap'n Jackie's hand, a little more roughly this time. Then she looked up and stopped. The Captain's eyes were still closed. A wet line glistened, running from her eye to the corner of her mouth. "Cap'n Jackie? Are you okay?"

That nurse would be back any second. Would they call the police on her? She set the key on Cap'n Jackie's lap under her limp hands and dashed to the door. Poking her head out, she checked down the hall. The coast was clear.

"I'm sorry, Cap'n Jackie." She whispered loud

so the Captain could hear, even with her back turned. "I'm really sorry!"

Tash took off at a fast walk, keeping close to the wall. The ghostie-man was still at it, his soft hooting growing louder as she walked. She tried not to see, but at the last second the *hoo-hoo* pulled her in. The empty eyes were right there, looking everywhere and nowhere.

Tash broke into a run and turned sharp at the first corner, away from the ghostie-man. She'd never gone this way. She hoped the hall didn't dead-end. The *hoo-hoo* faded as she took another turn and spotted an EXIT sign. When she pushed through the door and broke out into daylight, Tash found herself in an unfamiliar, smaller parking lot. She must be on the other side of the building.

Tash ran along the sidewalk. The ghostie-man's pale-lipped *hoo-hoo* echoed in the back of her mind, nipping at her heels. She tore around the corner and saw the familiar front parking lot. She stopped and leaned over with her hands on her knees, sucking air. Sweat trickled from her forehead.

She had never seen Cap'n Jackie cry before. *Never.* Not one time, not even when Mulligan died. The key

132

was supposed to *fix* things. Why didn't it work? And what did that twice for no *mean*?

Was it *no Tash*? Was she mad at Tash forever and ever? Not friends anymore? Tash wished she'd never thrown the key. Never left for camp without making up. She really, really wished she'd sent that sorry letter right away. But it was too late. She'd wrecked everything.

REAL

WORLD

Tash used the end of her T-shirt to wipe off her face. The coast was clear—no sign of anyone looking for her. But the Tigger nurse had probably called a security guard, or maybe even the police. She had to get out of there. Because what if they called Kevin, or what if he came home early and she wasn't there? He wouldn't trust her, and things would be ruined with him, too.

She circled to the far side, crouching behind parked cars. When she came to the last one, she ran for the street.

"Hey! Hey, Tash!"

That was Naomi's voice, but Tash didn't even look. Her mom might be with her.

"Tash?"

I don't care, I don't care. Tash's sneakers stomped the words across the asphalt, onto the cement sidewalk, past the barking dog, *Who cares?*, past the park, *I don't care.* The breeze whispered through her ears, *hoo-hoo, hoo-hoo.*

Tash ran all the way to Lake Street. The bus was coming, but the DON'T WALK sign was lit and if it didn't change, she'd miss that bus. She pounded the button for pedestrian crossing and the light turned to WALK just as the bus pulled up to the stop. Tash ran across the street, got on, and dropped her quarters in. She found an empty seat and sat staring out the window as the stores and restaurants and car repair places whizzed by.

That key drop? Sure as certain, that was a rager. Just like Tash's. It was a silent-treatment throw.

"*What goes around comes around,*" Cap'n Jackie liked to say. "*When you're not looking, it'll roll around and bop you upside the head.*"

But Cap'n Jackie said in her letter that everything was okay, that she loved Tash. So why was she mad?

Why was she crying? Why was she being a quitter? The questions burned circles around and around in Tash's head. She got off at her stop, jogged down the alley and into the back driveway. *Okay, whew.* Terkel wasn't there.

Tash let herself in and trudged up the stairs. If Cap'n Jackie was still mad about her throwing the key, that wasn't fair. Tash had apologized. But—wait. Maybe Cap'n Jackie had never gotten that letter. When had Tash sent it? She couldn't remember.

She unlocked the door to a nobody-home hush. Kevin should be coming in less than an hour. That was almost no time at all. Tash went back to her own room, made her bed, and picked some things up off the floor. She stepped to the window and looked, as she always had, to Cap'n Jackie's house. The house was quiet, shuttered and curtained. What if it stayed empty? What if Cap'n Jackie had to stay at White Oaks and she ended up like the ghostie-man?

Tash put her hands over her ears to shut off the echoes of *hoo-hoo.* Those ghostie-man eyes were so blank, nobody home, never home again. Even with her hands over her ears, Tash heard the *tink* of the key falling on the cold linoleum floor. *Hoo-hoo* and

136

tink and the ghostie-man's eyes and the finger lifting to tap once-twice—*NO*.

Cap'n Jackie wasn't coming back. Even if she did, it wouldn't be the same. Everybody leaves, everybody.

Tash grabbed her arms around herself, holding hard. She stomped her feet on the floor, but it didn't help. She was ALONE. She began to shake, rattling from the inside out and the outside in. Her brain stopped working. She dropped to the floor, crept into her closet, and curled into a tiny ball in the corner, eyes closed and hands over her ears. Shhh. Shhh.

"Tash?"

The bedroom door opened. Tash tried to catch her breath to speak, but all that came out was a little gasp.

"Tash, are you here?"

Suddenly Kevin was there on the floor with her, all around her.

"Oh, Bug. Oh, my little Bug, come here."

She ducked into his arms like a four-year-old Bug. She shivered and shook, freezing on the inside. Kevin held her tighter. "Shhhh. Shhh, baby. We're okay. Shhh." The shivering slowed, stopped. Started again. Kevin rocked Tash until her teeth quit rattling. Then

137

he made her breathe with him. "In, hold it. Out slow. In, hold it. Out slow."

Finally, Tash took a deep, quivery breath and pulled loose. Kevin tipped her chin up to look into her eyes.

"Bug, where's my phone? Why didn't you call me?"

Tash had forgotten all about the phone. She pulled it from her pocket and gave it to Kevin.

"Why is it on Do Not Disturb?" he asked.

Tash didn't answer. She curled back into Kevin's lap. She was too big to be hiding in the closet, too big to sit on his lap. She should tell him everything. But he'd be mad. He'd think he couldn't trust her. And besides, what would she tell him? How could she explain it?

"Bug? I tried calling twice from the Jam, and you didn't answer." Kevin's voice was gentle, quiet, questioning. Not mad. "Why did you put it on Do Not Disturb?"

"I don't know," she said. "I guess I was just playing with it."

Lying to Kevin felt awful. Worse than awful. He brushed her hair back and kissed the top of her head. He didn't believe her, but Kevin was Kevin. He pulled her out to the kitchen with him.

Tash sat at the table while he opened the fridge and turned on the stove. A few minutes later, he set a grilled cheese sandwich in front of her. She shook her head, pushing the plate away.

"One bite," said Kevin. "Just one. Because who makes the best grilled cheese?"

She took one bite. It was true. Kevin did make the best grilled cheese. She got that bite down, and then another.

"That's better," he said. "When you're done, we'll go see the Captain."

Tash pushed the plate away again.

"I don't think she even knows we're there," she said. "So maybe it doesn't matter if we go."

Kevin turned from the dishes and leaned on the sink. He folded his arms over his chest, studying Tash. Tash looked down at the table.

"Yesterday?" he asked. "When you had private time with her? Did something scare you?"

Tash shook her head. She wasn't lying. Nothing happened during that time.

"Maybe this is all just too much for you," said Kevin. "Is that it?"

Tash nodded. Her eyes watered, but she gritted

her teeth and swallowed hard, and the water went away.

"Tell you what," said Kevin. "You can stay in the lobby with the birds while I go down and say hello. Maybe once you get there, you'll feel like coming down, just for a minute or two. Just to say hi. Okay?"

"Do I have to?" asked Tash.

"Maybe not to Cap'n Jackie's room," said Kevin. "But you need to come along. You've had enough alone time today."

Good point. Tash, still with her eyes on the table, nodded.

"Go wash your face," said Kevin. "Then we'll go."

THE

CAPTAIN

HATES

A LIAR

Tash ran water on the washcloth and looked at herself in the mirror. She didn't like who she saw in there.

"*I hate a liar.*" Cap'n Jackie used to say that. "*You're not a liar, Kid. One of your best features. That Nathan, he used to shade the truth sometimes, but not you.*" She had definitely shaded the truth to Kevin, and left some major things out.

So now what? When she'd made her plan, she hadn't thought about after. She'd only gotten as far as giving Cap'n Jackie the key, and the magic happening, and everything being okay.

Everything was not okay.

Terkel took them to White Oaks much faster than the bus had. Tash wished it would take longer. Forever longer. She held her breath as she followed Kevin through the sliding glass doors into the lobby. No Naomi there, no book. Just the birds. Tash slumped into a chair.

"Do you want me to tell Cap'n Jackie anything?" asked Kevin.

"Nope."

He gave her a quizzical look, one eyebrow up.

"That Kevin, he's no fool," Cap'n Jackie used to say.

Cap'n Jackie was right.

"Come down when you feel like it," said Kevin.

Tash nodded. At least if Cap'n Jackie wasn't talking, she couldn't tell Kevin anything. That nurse would, though.

Tash watched the birds flit from one post to the other. Tweeting and chirping. She got up and put her nose on the glass. They didn't care. They just went on about their little birdie business.

"Do you hate it in here?" asked Tash. "Tap once for yes. Twice for no."

Nobody tapped.

"Hey." Naomi came up beside her. "Are you okay?"

Tash nodded. They stood shoulder-to-shoulder in front of the glass.

"There was a big fuss after you ran out." Naomi spoke in a low voice. "My mom grilled me. She thinks I was involved, but she can't prove it. I admitted under questioning that I knew you'd been here, but I didn't say anything else."

Tash nodded again.

"Because actually, I don't know anything else. What happened down there?"

Tash shrugged.

"You must have run into Susan, the nurse with blond hair and a big fake smile? She said you have a smart mouth."

Tash nodded.

"I've been accused of having a smart mouth, too," said Naomi. "I can never figure out why adults think that's a bad thing. It seems to me like a good thing."

The birds didn't seem to mind them being close to the glass at all. Maybe they thought everything outside the glass was like TV, not the real world.

"Are you mad?" Naomi asked. "Did I do something wrong?"

"No." Tash turned away from the glass and flopped

into one of the chairs. "Sorry I took off without saying anything. I just—well—things didn't go the way I wanted them to."

Naomi sat down, too.

"I suppose they'll tell Kevin I was here," said Tash.

"They will."

"Those birds." Tash pointed at the cage. "Have you ever seen them take a dead one out?"

Naomi shook her head.

"Have you ever seen them take a dead person out of here?" asked Tash.

"No," said Naomi. "That mostly happens in that south wing I told you about."

"Have you been there?"

"Yup. It's like here without the birds. Nurses, rooms, people in wheelchairs. A fish tank."

The birds had zero privacy. One bird was crammed back in the little hidey-hole nest as far as it could go. It didn't even stick its beak out. Maybe that was the one who didn't like people standing close to the glass.

"I don't like that wing," said Naomi. "The people are different. There's a few who are out of it here, but over there almost everyone is. It's way too sad, and also a little bit creepy."

Maybe because there weren't any birds over there? Although Tash hadn't seen any of the patients hanging around by the birds here. If she were stuck in this place, she'd want to be by the birds all the time.

"So what happened before?" Naomi asked. "Did you talk to Cap'n Jackie?"

"We sort of had a fight," said Tash.

"She talked?" Naomi popped up in her chair. "That's good, right?"

"No. She doesn't need to talk to fight."

Naomi tipped her head.

"Trust me," said Tash.

"Kevin's coming," said Naomi.

Tash slunk down in the chair. Kevin came around to the other side of it.

"Hello, Naomi the bird manager," he said.

"The what?"

"Bird manager?" He pointed at the glass. "In charge of them?"

"Ha, ha," said Tash. "Naomi, this is Kevin."

"Hi, Kevin," said Naomi.

"Hi, Naomi. Good to officially meet you," he said. "Tash, will you come with me?"

As Tash got up, Naomi gave her a sympathetic look. Just past the crowded dining room, Kevin waited for her to catch up. He put his hands on her shoulders and looked her in the eye.

"I understand you were here this morning."

Tash looked down at the tiled floor.

"We'll talk about that more when we get home. For now, I want you to come down and see Cap'n Jackie."

"Did she say something?" Tash looked up quick. "Did she tell you I was here?"

"No. She's still not talking. Tash, you need to tell me what happened."

Tash didn't even know how to start.

"Did you get mad at her?" asked Kevin.

"Sort of."

Kevin sighed.

"Was it a rager?"

"No, Kevin! It wasn't, not like that. I mean . . ."

She looked down again, remembering Cap'n Jackie's hand moving, stretching out, and deliberately dropping the key.

146

"It seemed like she was the one who was mad."

"Did she say something?"

"No."

"How could you tell she was mad?"

"I could tell," said Tash.

"She's the only one who can top you at that game," said Kevin. "Come on. If she's mad, we'll work it out. But one way or another, you need to show up."

"That nurse hates me," Tash said in a small voice.

"This is not about that nurse. Come on."

PROMISE

Tash hung back in the doorway of Cap'n Jackie's room.

"Hey, Captain," Kevin said. "Look who I found."

Tash searched the floor as she entered, in case Cap'n Jackie had dropped the key somewhere. The Captain was lying flat on her back in bed, pale and perfectly still. Tash took a close look at the black leather seat of the wheelchair to see if the key was there.

"Come over here, Tash," said Kevin. "Talk to the Captain."

Kevin scooted the chair right next to the bed. He stood behind it. Tash sat, looking closely at Cap'n Jackie. The blanket rose and fell, ever so slightly.

"Hi, Cap'n Jackie." Her voice shook in that way she hated. "I'm here."

Cap'n Jackie didn't open her eyes. She didn't move at all. Her face was still as still could be. Her left hand was under the blanket. The right one was on her stomach.

"Please do what they say so you can come home," said Tash. "I'll wash the dishes every day. I'll follow orders all the time."

She looked up at Kevin again. He nodded slowly. His eyes were shiny.

"Cap'n Jackie?" he said. "I'm going to step out into the hall for a few minutes. I think maybe Tash has some things to say to you in private."

The second the door closed behind Kevin, Tash lifted the blanket and looked in Cap'n Jackie's left hand. It was empty.

"Where's the key?" she whispered. "If you don't want it anymore, that's okay, but I think maybe I need it."

Nothing from Cap'n Jackie. Not even a twitch.

Tash dropped to her knees on the floor. She searched the bare tile in every direction. After checking the tops of the dresser and nightstand, she returned to Cap'n Jackie.

"Maybe you never got my letter. The one where I said I was sorry for throwing the key in the first place."

Cap'n Jackie's face was perfectly still. Was she asleep for real?

"And for being a little stinker."

A tiny movement caught Tash's eye. She held her breath and stared at Cap'n Jackie's right hand.

"Was that once for yes?" she whispered. "Yes, I'm a little stinker? Or yes, you got the letter?"

Nothing.

"Just come home, okay? I won't ever be a little stinker again."

"Tash?" Kevin opened the door a crack.

"I promise," Tash whispered. "No more little stinker."

"The nurse is coming in."

"Kevin, I think she tapped once for yes."

"Really?" Kevin walked over and took Cap'n Jackie's hand in his. "Captain?"

Nothing. Not a twitch of finger or eyelid.

"I thought I saw it," said Tash. "I mean, I wasn't looking right at her hand like before, but I thought it twitched."

"I hope you're right," said Kevin. "Cap'n Jackie, Nathan will be here tomorrow. His flight gets in around nine. We'll all meet here and see what we can figure out."

A nurse came in. Not the Tigger one and not the good one. A new one.

"See you tomorrow," Tash whispered.

She stayed close to Kevin on the way out, keeping her head tucked so none of the nurses would notice her. They found Naomi in the lobby.

"Wait," Tash told Kevin. "I want to talk to Naomi for a sec."

"I'll be out by the car," said Kevin.

He headed out the doors and Tash sat across from Naomi.

"How'd it go?" asked Naomi.

"I don't know." Tash shook her head. "I think *maybe* we're not fighting anymore. It's hard to tell."

"Will you be back tomorrow?"

"Yup. With Nathan."

"Who's Nathan?"

"Cap'n Jackie's nephew."

"See you tomorrow, then?"

Tash nodded and headed out to the car. Key or no, she felt a tiny bit better. Like maybe she and Cap'n Jackie had made up. She'd made a promise. No more little stinker. She'd keep it.

ONCE

FOR

YES

Lightning flickered through the evening like a faulty light, off and on, off and on. Tash had very little to say through dinner. Kevin asked a couple of questions, but he didn't push it. When Tash finally put on her pajamas and crawled between the sheets, Kevin sat on the edge of the bed. He brushed his hand across her forehead, tucking her hair back.

"Kevin, I think she's going to be okay. I really do."

"I hope you're right, Bug." Kevin looked out the window. "Nathan will be here tomorrow, and we'll figure things out."

It was hard for Tash to think about Nathan as someone who could figure anything out. Even though he was a grown-up, she mostly knew him from Cap'n Jackie's stories where he was a kid. Her only real-life memories of him were from his last visit two years ago. He stayed in her room at Cap'n Jackie's for three days and called her Kidlet and laughed too loud.

She hoped he hadn't seen what she wrote on the wall of that room. And what if the nurse at White Oaks complained to him about her?

"What did that nurse say about me?" Tash's voice was small, afraid.

"A lot about the rules and why children aren't allowed to visit alone," he said. "You made me look bad, you know. Wandering around the city on your own."

"Sorry," said Tash, and she meant it.

"Do you want to tell me what actually happened?" asked Kevin.

"I snuck in. I talked to Cap'n Jackie and she wouldn't answer, and I kinda got a little bit mad. Then she got mad. Then the nurse came in."

"How do you know she got mad? Did she say something?"

Tash took a deep breath.

"I gave her something," she said. "Something she

gave me once. I gave it back to her, and she dropped it. On purpose. Like this."

She showed him the deliberate raising of the fist and opening of the hand.

"Huh." Kevin shook his head. "Well, you got more life out of her than anyone else has. That might be a good thing."

Tash fiddled with the edge of the sheet. Kevin probably knew she was talking about the key. She'd left it in her pocket once, and it went in the laundry. When she came home from school that day, the key was on her nightstand.

"I didn't mean to make her cry," she said.

"She cried?"

"One tear." Tash traced the path down her own face. "Like this."

"Sometimes crying is really, really good."

"I wish she'd just act like herself," said Tash. "Why won't she?"

"I don't know," said Kevin. "Doesn't seem like the folks at White Oaks know quite what's wrong, either. It's hard when we know what's good for someone but they don't know it's good and they don't want to do it."

He kept looking at Tash, and she waited for him to say it, but he didn't. So then she had to.

"Like me going to camp," she said.

He nodded, and brushed her forehead again.

"Yes," he said. "I was able to make you. But we can't make Cap'n Jackie."

Low thunder growled outside. Raindrops spatted against the window. Kevin circled the foot of Tash's bed and pushed it closed.

"Get some sleep," he said. "Tomorrow's a new day. Maybe the Captain really does know what's best. Nathan's been researching home care options."

"Really?" Tash sat up straight. "Really, can that happen? Because Kevin, I bet that would work. Maybe it's just the strangers she hates, and if she comes home she'll be fine. Hey, I know! We could pay Naomi's mom to come and help her at home."

"We'll see," said Kevin. "Now get some sleep."

Tash jerked out of a half-formed dream. Rain hammered the roof, but that wasn't what had woken her. It was something else. She listened hard in the darkness.

TINK.

Tash whirled and stared at the window. She sat up, leaning close to the glass. A streetlight cast a glow across the space between houses. Raindrops broke the light up, scattering the edges and shapes.

TINK.

Tash jumped back. Something was clinking on the window. She stared at the rivulets dripping down the glass, then moved closer and looked down into the side yard. Maybe someone was throwing rocks. Nope, nobody there.

What made that sound? Hail, maybe? Cap'n Jackie's house hulked in the dark. The maple in the side yard thrashed in the wind. Branches and twigs cast shifting shadow patterns, and the streetlight continued to glow.

Tash rapped her knuckles very softly on the glass.

Tap, tap.

Tink.

Ever so soft. Like a quiet argument. Yes, no, yes.

Tash's heart thumped hard. The leaf-shadows shifted and danced, kaleidoscope patterns of moony light and rain-washed dark. Tash reached out, twice-tapped again, and waited. This time, no answer. She tried again. *Tap tap?*

Drops ran down the glass. Tash pushed the window up a few inches, and a cool breeze and mist of rain came in.

She slid back into bed and leaned against the headboard, pulling the quilt up around her shoulders. Nothing moved; nothing tapped. The rain was quieter now, the wind a breath instead of a blow. Tash's eyes were so heavy. She blinked and forced them open. Blinked again, closing them just for a minute, just to rest . . .

MIXING

UP

MAGIC

The sun blasted Tash's eyes open. A bird chirped just outside her window. The rain and the dark were long gone. But that tapping . . . ? That wasn't a dream, was it? It had been so clear. As clear as that bird chirp.

Tash scrambled out of bed and opened the window as far as it would go. Sidewalks were drying and the grass sparkled bright. A pan banged in the kitchen. A drawer opened and closed. It was Thursday, Kevin's day off. Nathan came today. Today, they'd figure out how to get Cap'n Jackie home. Maybe she'd even be home by this time tomorrow.

Tash lay back in bed. This time yesterday, she'd been on her way to White Oaks. Even though yesterday hadn't gone the way she'd wanted, the fight with

Cap'n Jackie—if that's what it was—had felt a little bit good. Certainly better than that blank-eyed zero stuff. She and Cap'n Jackie had always fought. It was one of the things they did together.

Most of their fights went the same way. They'd get into it over something, they'd yell back and forth, and then Tash would stomp off to her room. Cap'n Jackie would leave Tash alone while she did her own thing in the kitchen, plenty loud enough to hear through a closed door.

Heavy footsteps. Banging drawers and slamming cupboards. Fridge open, fridge closed. Maybe some muttering about rotten little stinkers with no manners. After a while the mixer would rev up and drown out the muttering. There'd be more banging around, water running, and then the oven door would open and close.

Eventually a warm, sweet smell would slide under the bedroom door and shimmy into Tash's nose, soothing and settling. It smelled like *I'll make up if you'll make up*. It smelled like *Maybe it's time for sorries*.

Then there'd be footsteps and a *THUD THUD tap-ta-tap* on the door. If Tash was still mad, she might use the side of her fist to hammer *TWICE! FOR! NO!* on the wall.

On the other side of the door, there'd come a tiny *tap* for yes, and then Cap'n Jackie's footsteps would fade back to the kitchen. Tash would open the door a crack and pull the plate in. She'd burned her mouth on hot cookies more than once.

Then she'd go out to the kitchen and, without a word, start to wash the dirty dishes in the sink. The Captain would dry, and when the dishes were all put away, they'd sit down at the kitchen table and talk.

Cookies were the only thing Cap'n Jackie was good for in the kitchen. She said so herself. She said it was less baking and more magic-potion-mixing. She didn't even use a recipe, just threw around flour and butter and eggs and some love and respect and friendship. That's what she said.

"Kevin!" called Tash.

Kevin poked his head into her room.

"Can I make some cookies for Cap'n Jackie?" she asked.

"Great idea," he said. "But eat some breakfast before you start in on the cookie dough. Those raw eggs came right out of a chicken's butt, you know."

"Kevin, that's gross."

"So is salmonella. Pancakes or omelet?"

"Omelet, please."

After breakfast, Tash found Kevin's cookbook and looked up a recipe for chocolate-chip cookies. It wouldn't be the same as Cap'n Jackie's, but it might be close enough. Kevin helped her find the ingredients, then went to his bedroom to pay bills. Tash set the oven to preheat and carefully followed the recipe, step by step. She wished she had the key to help with the magic potion part.

She cracked eggs and stirred and mixed. Once the flour was in, the batter didn't taste like raw eggs at all. More like cold cookies. She dropped dollops of dough in three columns on parchment paper and put the cookie sheet in the oven. A few minutes later, the smell of making up and getting back to normal spread across the apartment.

Tash felt very hopeful as she washed the mixing bowl, measuring cups, and beaters. The cookies were just the thing. A booster shot of magic. Cap'n Jackie might even be home by this afternoon, and bring the key with her.

The timer dinged and Tash pulled out the first batch. They looked just fine. A little flatter than Cap'n

Jackie's, maybe, but they should still work. She was scooping them off the cookie sheet and onto the cooling rack when Kevin's phone rang.

"Oh, no. Oh, Nathan."

Tash stopped breathing and listened hard.

"Nathan, I'm so sorry. Where are you now? Do you need a ride?"

Tash left the kitchen and stood in Kevin's bedroom doorway, spatula still in her hand. Kevin glanced briefly at her, then looked out the window.

"Okay. Sure. Text me when you're on your way."

Kevin put the phone down. Tash waited, suddenly aware of how loud her heart was beating. Kevin turned to face her.

"Tash, baby."

Tash shook her head. No.

"Come here."

Tash shook her head again and took a step back.

"Tash, that was Nathan."

She didn't decide to throw the spatula. It just sort of happened. It flew across the room and hit Kevin's closet door. Tash turned and ran and slammed the door to her bedroom. No. No. Twice for no. She backed up to the door, holding it closed.

"Bug."

Kevin's tapping was gentle on her door. Not once, not twice, no secret pattern, but a run of soft little *tap-a-taps*.

"Is it better if I talk from out here?" he asked.

"No."

Tash slid to the floor, still with her back against the door.

"That was Nathan," Kevin said. "He just landed. When he turned his phone on, he had a message from White Oaks."

"No, he didn't!" yelled Tash.

Kevin didn't say anything.

"He's a liar!" said Tash. "Even Cap'n Jackie says so!"

"Tasha, baby. My Natasha."

Kevin had the softest voice in the world. Way softer than Cap'n Jackie's voice ever was. Cap'n Jackie would say, *Get yourself up off of that floor and face facts, Kiddo.* She'd say, *Stand up and take it on the chin.* She'd say, *Give Kevin a break for once.*

Tash closed her eyes, gritted her teeth. Took a breath in and a breath out. Then she stood and opened the door.

"Okay." She lifted her chin up and looked Kevin in the eye. "What did Nathan say?"

PART THREE

TAKING

IT ON

THE

CHIN

Captain Jackie died in the middle of the night.

Kevin's slow, careful words chugged past Tash's ears like a sluggish freight train, car by car, each carrying a heavy load. Nothing anyone could do. Maybe a blood clot. Lungs. Not enough movement, sometimes happens. Peaceful, not painful. Embolism? Nathan says no autopsy. Won't change anything. Nothing change. Won't change.

Kevin's voice continued, but Tash's mind headed down a different track. Gone like Mulligan. Gone and gone and gone. Alone. Empty house, empty and always.

"Tasha, baby?"

Kevin's voice came through the empty like a train whistle in the night. Long distance like cookies in the mail, like letters never sent, never opened, never read.

"Tash?"

Tash turned around and backed into Kevin, crossing her arms over her chest. He put both of his arms around her and held her tight. They stood like that in silence, for a long time.

KEYLESS

Kevin and Tash waited for Nathan on Cap'n Jackie's back steps.

"Those berries need to be picked," said Kevin. "The birds are getting them all."

Tash thought of the little finches in the glass cage at White Oaks. She wished she could take them some raspberries. Or better yet, open the door. Let them fly free and get their own raspberries.

"Kevin," she said.

"Yes, Tash?"

"I should've made the cookies sooner. Maybe she would've gotten better."

"I don't think so, babe. I think she made up her mind to go. You know when Cap'n Jackie makes up her mind, nobody can stop her."

"Do you think she's mad at me for not bringing cookies?"

Kevin looked down at her. His eyes were so sad.

"I mean, maybe she was just waiting for some cookies. Maybe that's what would have changed everything."

"I don't think it works like that."

"I don't want her to be mad at me. It seemed like she wasn't so much when we left yesterday. Do you think she was?"

"Bug, I don't think she's mad at you. Not in any possible way."

Kevin pulled Tash close. She leaned into him.

"She might be," she said. "If you can stay mad after you die."

"Even if you can, she wouldn't," said Kevin. "I think she's loving you without one drop of mad."

A car pulled into the alley and parked in Cap'n Jackie's driveway. The car door closed gently, as if the driver were trying not to wake anyone. Nathan came through the garage and stepped into the yard.

He looked smaller than last time Tash had seen him. Now he wasn't much taller than her. His clothes were neatly pressed, slacks and a polo shirt, bright yellow against his dark skin. Grown-up leather shoes and a brown leather bag slung over his shoulder. Hair buzzed close to the scalp. Enormous dark-brown eyes.

Kevin walked to Nathan, hand out. They shook hands and Kevin pulled Nathan into a hug. Tash stood but stayed on the porch steps, watching. Finally, Nathan stepped back and looked at her.

"Hi, Kid," he said.

"I broke that window." Tash pointed to the back door. "The door was locked."

"She's Tash now," said Kevin. "Not Kid."

"Tash." Nathan nodded.

Tash stepped aside as he walked up the steps, and she and Kevin followed him into the kitchen. He shrugged off his bag and set it on the kitchen counter.

"Looks like you did a good job of cleaning up the glass," he said.

Two years ago, Tash had decided she didn't like Nathan the first time he'd called her Kidlet. That's when she'd started thinking of him as Naaythan, although she'd never called him that to his face. Cap'n

Jackie got really mad when she said it out loud, so she mostly kept it to herself. He'd better not call her Kidlet. He'd better not even call her Kid again.

Nathan suddenly took a breath so big, it was like sucking all the air out of the room. He held it a moment, then collapsed in one of the kitchen chairs. Kevin sat next to him, reached over and put his hand on Nathan's.

"We're right here," he said. "We're right here with you."

Nathan shook his head, looking down at the table. A drop fell on the wood, and then another. Tash was horrified and impressed and embarrassed. He was crying, right there in front of them. Not even trying to hide it.

"That Nathan, he's too sensitive to be in this world."

"What about me?" Tash had asked. "I'm sensitive."

Cap'n Jackie had smiled.

"Yes, you are, but you're fierce in a way that Nathan never quite manages. You'll be okay, my Kid. It's the world that needs to look out for you."

"I can't believe she left us." Nathan's voice trembled all over the place. "I was so sure she'd snap out of it."

"I know." Kevin spoke in the same quiet voice he

used with Tash when she was upset. "I know. We thought so, too."

It wasn't fair. Why did Nathan have to cry like that? His long eyelashes were spiky wet. Even Kevin's eyes were wet. Why'd everybody have to *cry*, anyway? Crying never did anybody any good, never, not one time!

Kevin pushed a chair out with his foot and nodded toward it. Tash shook her head. Kevin lowered his eyebrows, looked at the chair, then at Nathan. Tash shook her head again. So what if she *was* a little stinker? So what? Cap'n Jackie was dead, so who cared? Nobody, that's who!

She walked away. Out the back door. Down the porch steps.

"Tash, come back here," said Kevin.

Tash scooted through the hedge and ran up the stairs. She slammed the door behind her and paced around the kitchen. She was sad too, and nobody cared. She was way sadder than Kevin *or* stupid Nathan. They were grown-ups; they didn't need Cap'n Jackie. They didn't have any right to cry.

Why didn't she cry? What was wrong with her? She's the one who should be crying. She was sensitive, too. Wasn't she?

The single pan of cookies was still laid out on the cooling rack. Kevin had put everything else away and turned the oven off. Tash picked up a cookie. It wasn't magic. It was *stupid*. She crushed the cookie in her fist and threw it on the floor. Magic was stupid. There was no such thing as magic.

She picked up another cookie and threw it at the sink. Stupid cookies didn't do any good at *all*. She threw another one, and then another. The very last one she held in her hand, and she hated it for being wrong. Too flat. She took a bite, and it was nothing like Cap'n Jackie's cookies. She spit it out, trying to get the taste off her tongue. The next spit turned into a gag followed by a sob that shook her whole body.

Water began to leak out of her eyes, way too much to swallow back. Tears bigger and wetter than Nathan's. More and more water, a rainstorm, a river, a waterfall. Tash was a twig going under. She tried to catch her breath, and that just made her cry harder.

If only she had the key. If she had the key, she could hold it and make everything be different. Without the key, she didn't have anything. Not one single thing. She crumpled to the floor and scooted tight into the corner.

The side door slammed shut, and footsteps came up

the stairs. Tash wiped her face and tried to stop crying. Kevin better not bring Nathan with him. He'd just better not. He'd better not put on sad eyes and talk about how we need to think about other people's feelings.

She didn't care about Kevin's sad eyes and she didn't care about Nathan. She didn't care about anything. Nothing at all. Nothing, nothing, nothing. She put her head down on her knees and squeezed her eyes shut.

The door opened and footsteps fell across the floor. Why didn't Kevin say anything? He was right there. She could hear him breathing.

What if it wasn't Kevin?

Tash lifted her head just enough to peek. It was Kevin. He was sitting on the floor in front of the fridge, legs drawn up, head on his arms.

"Kevin?"

He lifted his head and met her eyes. And yes, they were sad eyes. But not the kind that tried to make her do something.

"Yes?"

"What are you doing?"

"Being with you."

Tash dropped her head back down because the tears were still coming. Lots of them.

A

GIFT

Tash had never been so tired in her whole life. Kevin carried her to bed, and she did not complain. She barely remembered sliding between the sheets. Kevin's hand was cool on her forehead.

"Shhhhh, shhhh, go to sleep, my Bug. I'll be right here."

He was, too. She woke in the early evening, had some soup, and went back to sleep. The next thing she knew, the apartment was dark and quiet. Tash sat up and looked out the window at Cap'n Jackie's house.

Dead. What did that even mean, dead? Was she truly gone? Gone forever and ever? How could there be no more Cap'n Jackie? The only person Tash knew personally who had died was Mulligan the cat. And even if Cap'n Jackie did claim he was still in the house, as far as Tash could see, Mullie was just plain gone. She'd never seen him again. Not one time.

The window was open and the cool of the summer night came through. Tash leaned her forehead against the glass. What would happen to her? Would she just have to stay alone now, all the time? Every day? Could she do it?

She got back into bed, pulling the sheets and the blanket up, wrapping them around her. She wished Mulligan were here. Why didn't he come and see her? If Tash was so full of magic like Cap'n Jackie always said, why couldn't she make them both show up right here, right now?

She squeezed her eyes shut. *When I wake up, I'll be at Cap'n Jackie's, and Mulligan will be in the bed with me, and the Captain will come in and wake me up, and I'll have a bowl of cereal and some cinnamon toast, and . . .*

A hand on her forehead woke her and Tash turned, so happy to be at Cap'n Jackie's and . . . no.

"Tash?" said Kevin. "I was getting worried about you. You slept so long."

Tash rolled away, pulling the blanket over her head.

"You need to get up and eat something. Here, I brought you a glass of water."

As if a glass of water could fix anything.

Tash moved from the bedroom to the living-room couch. She lay there, wrapped in a different blanket, staring at the ceiling. She hadn't even been there ten minutes when Kevin's phone rang.

"Yes, she's up. Mmm-hm. Yes. Rough night, of course."

"Don't tell him anything about me!" Tash whispered.

Kevin raised his eyebrows.

"Yes," he said into the phone. "She'll be there." He set the phone down. "Nathan will be over at Cap'n Jackie's in about fifteen minutes."

"No."

"Yes."

"I'm too tired."

"Come on. Get dressed. I'll walk you over."

Kevin and Tash sat in silence on Cap'n Jackie's back steps. When Nathan arrived, Kevin got up and gave him a hug. Then he went out through the garage. Tash felt very, very small sitting alone on the bottom step.

"Hi, Tash," said Nathan.

At least he didn't call her Kidlet. At least he was in shorts and a T-shirt, and not so New-Yorky looking. He sat on the step next to her. Tash stared at her feet. Nathan reached into his bag and pulled out two envelopes.

"These were with Cap'n Jackie's things," he said.

The top envelope was addressed to Cap'n Jackie in Tash's handwriting. It had never been opened.

"She never got it?" Tash asked.

"I took her mail to the hospital, but she never opened any of it," said Nathan.

That's why Cap'n Jackie was so mad. She didn't even know Tash had apologized. Well, that wasn't fair. Tash had written it. It wasn't her fault Cap'n Jackie hadn't opened it. Tash looked at the second envelope. This one had *Natasha K. McCorry* on the front in Cap'n Jackie's perfect cursive writing. She had said she learned it at Catholic school.

"I got one, too," Nathan said. "You know what a rager is?"

Tash wanted to say *duh*, but instead she just nodded.

"Cap'n Jackie pitched one at me when she woke up after the surgery, before she started the silent treatment. My letter was written that night. Probably she wrote yours then, too."

Nathan's eyes were big and clear, and so brown. At least they weren't all wet this time.

"What did your letter say?" asked Tash.

Nathan tipped his head slightly to the side, and his eyes narrowed a tiny bit. One corner of his mouth came up. Much better than the fake-friendly-to-the-little-kid smile he usually gave her.

"That's between me and Cap'n Jackie," he said. "I have to go to the airport now and pick up Theo. We'll be back later this afternoon."

"Who's Theo?"

"He's my fiancé. I want him to meet you and Kevin."

"Why?"

"Because he's going to be family."

Nathan stood and put his hands in his pockets, then pulled one out.

"One more thing," he said, opening his hand. "The custodian found this key with Cap'n Jackie's things. Do you know what it's to?"

180

The key lay on his palm. Tash twitched to reach for it but stopped. She looked up at Nathan, studying his face. If he knew Vanessa and Cap'n Jackie, he had to know about the key.

"You don't know what it is?" Tash asked.

"Never saw it before."

Tash took the key from him. She curled her fingers around it and felt the familiar shape, the warmth. She closed her eyes. Maybe when she opened them, Nathan would be gone. Maybe Cap'n Jackie would be there instead.

"Garden looks better than it did," said Nathan. "Did you do that?"

Tash opened her eyes. Not Cap'n Jackie. Just Nathan, waiting for her to open her eyes.

"I'll be back in a while with Theo."

As soon as Nathan disappeared through the garage, Tash tore the envelope open.

August 7

My Dear Kid,

Thank you for throwing the key at my head. I needed it more than you did. It was with me when I fell. I held it in my hand and I touched Draphin in the living flesh. She sang in my ear. I danced with Vanessa. Mulligan was there. It's time for me to go.

Nathan is trying to stop me but he can't. I'm done here. You'll miss me but you'll be fine. The key is the only Home Alone plan you need.

Things to remember:

1. Kevin is pure gold.

2. Keep raging. It makes you strong.

3. Don't be jealous of Nathan. You need each other. You're family.

4. You're never too old for magic.

Mulligan says meow. Draphin loves you and so do I. Watch out for Crocs.

YOUR CAPTAIN,
Jackie

WHEN

YOU NEED

SOME

MAGIC

Tash held the key tight in one hand and the letter in the other, reading it over and over again. The key was with Cap'n Jackie when she fell. The key made Draphin and Vanessa come and be with her, and she almost died. Then she got stuck in the hospital with no key. Then Tash gave her the key back, and then she died.

"When you need some magic, squeeze it tight. Draphin and Mulligan and I will have your back, and we'll take care of whatever's going on together. You won't be alone."

Tash squeezed the key tight and closed her eyes. She waited for somebody to have her back. Why didn't it work for her?

Clink. Tink.

Tash opened her eyes wide, remembering the tink-ing on the windowpane in the night. Had that been Cap'n Jackie? Maybe she was saying, *Yes, it worked. I'm leaving now.* But that wasn't how it was supposed to work. That wasn't what Tash wanted.

But it was Cap'n Jackie's key. She'd loaned it to Tash, but it was hers. It did what she wanted. She said it right there in the letter: *I'm done here.*

Done with this yard. Done with this house. Done with Tash. Cap'n Jackie wanted to be gone, and now she was gone and Tash was alone. But somehow, the alone felt different from before. She turned and walked up the steps and into Cap'n Jackie's kitchen. It was very, very empty, but the empty was just empty. It didn't try to grab her by the throat.

Tash's footsteps were the loudest thing in the house as she crossed the kitchen and dining room and went to stand before her own room. Still squeez-ing the key in one hand, she put her other hand on the doorknob. What if, when she opened the door, the wall wasn't there anymore? What if it was like her dream at camp, a big window with Draphin flying around outside?

She closed her eyes, turned the knob, and pushed the door open.

Opened her eyes.

YOU ARE NOT THE CAPTAIN OF ANYTHING.

Smack in the middle of the wall, big and loud. Tash wished with all of her heart that she had never, ever written that.

"I didn't mean it," she said out loud. "I really didn't."

Kevin turned from the counter as Tash came in the back door.

"How'd it go with Nathan?"

"It went okay."

"Your friend Naomi's mom called," said Kevin. "She said that she and Naomi are so sorry about Cap'n Jackie."

Tash had completely forgotten about Naomi, forgotten that she'd said she'd see her tomorrow and then never came back.

"They'd like to have you over sometime before school starts," said Kevin. "Would you like that?"

"I guess so," said Tash.

She couldn't really imagine school starting or going over to someone's house or anything that normal. It all seemed so far away.

"Kevin, can we go buy some paint and paint my wall at Cap'n Jackie's?"

"That house is Nathan's now. I don't know what he plans to do, if he's going to sell it or what."

"But if he sells it, then we really should paint the wall, right? Nobody wants to buy it with my little kid writing all over it."

"Well, that's a point. But we should ask him what color he wants."

"Can't we paint a coat over the writing before he gets back? Please?"

Kevin studied her for a few minutes longer, and then nodded.

"Tell you what. We'll go to the store and get some primer, and cover the wall with that. Then it'll be ready to paint however Nathan wants it."

Tash and Kevin pushed the furniture to the center of the room and covered the floor with some old sheets. Kevin showed Tash how to use the roller, and then he went to work taping the trim.

Tash eased the clean white foam roller into the primer and rolled it back and forth until the roller was saturated. Then she rolled it on the ridges of the paint pan so it wasn't drippy.

She took it directly to the patch of wall where she'd scrawled YOU ARE NOT THE CAPTAIN OF ANYTHING. It seemed like years and years ago she had done that. Kevin hadn't said one word about it. Kevin was good that way. The primer mostly covered it up, but not quite.

The guy at the paint store had said this was the best stuff for covering marker. And if they painted the room in a dark color, it should be okay. Tash painted over stick figures of her and Cap'n Jackie, Draphin, and Mulligan, watched them fade under the paint to where she could barely see them. She couldn't even remember making those tic-tac-toe squares in the corner. She did remember writing EVERYTHING IS STOOOOPID, though.

Tash stopped for a moment and closed her eyes. She could almost hear Cap'n Jackie muttering in the kitchen. She reached into her pocket and held the key and inhaled deeply. She'd never smell those cookies again. Not *those* cookies.

She opened her eyes and gave the key an extra

squeeze before picking up the roller again. As she painted, she thought about Cap'n Jackie's letter. *You need each other,* she'd said. *You're family.*

"Kevin?"

"Yes, Bug?"

"Why did Nathan live with Cap'n Jackie anyway? What happened to his parents?"

"The way I understand it, when Nathan was a teenager, he told his parents he was gay. They weren't very happy about it."

Kevin was done taping. He picked up the brush and started to paint around the one small window.

"Why not?" asked Tash.

"Sometimes parents aren't. So Nathan came to live with his aunt Vanessa."

"Did his parents make him?"

"Maybe. I don't know the details. But he lived here for almost four years and graduated high school here."

So Nathan had lived in this room for four whole years. He was probably never a little stinker. Never wrote stupid stuff on the walls. No wonder Cap'n Jackie liked him best. After Vanessa, of course.

Tash rolled over the *You are not the captain* part one more time. Then she started on the rest of the wall, connecting one patch of primer to the next. She rolled and rolled, covering everything she could reach.

"Hello!" Nathan called from the kitchen.

"Back here!" called Kevin.

Footsteps came through the dining room.

"A project!" Tash turned to see the source of a very deep voice that was not Nathan's. "Look, Nathan, it's a project!"

"Kevin, Tash, this is Theo," said Nathan. "Theo, Kevin and Tash."

"Hello." Theo was very thin and very tall. His skin was a lighter brown than Nathan's, and his head was shaved completely bald. "Tash, I'm so sorry for your loss."

Tash wasn't sure what to say to that. *Thank you? Me too?*

Theo reached out an enormous hand. Tash set the roller down and shook it. She had never shaken a hand that big. Theo turned to Kevin, who pulled him into a hug.

"Welcome," said Kevin. "We're glad you're here."

Nathan stood back with his arms crossed, smiling. It made him look young. Like someone who might have been a teenager.

"Nathan, I hope you don't mind," said Kevin. "Tash wanted to do some redecorating, so we thought we'd at least get the priming under way. I don't know what your plans are for the house."

Nathan and Theo looked at each other. Theo nodded, as if they had a secret no-words language.

"No decisions yet," said Nathan. "Not making any more decisions today."

"This looks like a perfect project," said Theo. "Tash, what color were you thinking?"

Theo looked to Tash very seriously, as if her opinion were the most important.

"Maybe something dark?" Tash had been thinking and thinking about the dream she'd had at camp, where the wall had turned into a nighttime window. Cap'n Jackie had looked so happy in that dream, and Draphin had been realer than real. "Dark purply blue? Like right after sunset?"

"I like that," said Theo. "A nice rich color. But it might make the room kind of dark. We'll need a light trim."

"I have an idea," said Nathan. "This big wall here — why don't we create a window?"

Tash, who'd been holding the key so its edges

pressed into her palm, whipped her head around to look at Nathan.

"What kind of window?" she asked.

"A magical window. We paint it so it looks just like a window frame, and then outside we can make any scene we want, with a moon and stars. That'll brighten things up a bit."

A tingle moved up from the key in Tash's hand, up her arm and into her heart.

"That Nathan, he can draw anything. You tell him an imagining, and slam-wham, it's on the paper."

She hadn't said anything about her dream or a window in the wall. Was Nathan a mind reader?

"Do you know who Draphin is?" she asked.

"Draphin?" Nathan shook his head no. "Theo, do you know Draphin?"

"I don't know any Draphin. Kevin, do you know someone named Draphin?"

"I've heard of Draphin." Kevin glanced sideways at Tash. "But never actually met her."

Tash felt the water creeping up behind her eyes again. Draphin and the Crocs, they were between her and Cap'n Jackie. Not Nathan's. Hers.

"You know Nathan's job is set design, don't you?"

asked Theo. "Anything you want outside that window, Nathan can make it."

Somehow when Theo talked about how great Nathan was, it wasn't so annoying. It was different coming out of this big, tall man with the deep, kind voice. When they'd shaken hands, Tash had accidentally gotten some primer on Theo's hand, but he didn't seem to mind.

Tash squeezed the key tighter. She didn't have to tell them anything. She could keep Draphin for her very own. But what if they really could make her dream slam-wham onto the wall? Cap'n Jackie would probably like it. She'd probably like it a lot.

ENDINGS

AND

BEGINNINGS

Kevin and Theo went off to buy paint, with a list of colors that Tash and Theo had put together. Shades of blue and purple, indigo plus some glitter for Draphin's eyes, gold and green for dragon wings and dragon-flies, gray for the dolphin tail, silver and white for the moon, black for Mulligan and Cap'n Jackie's silhouettes, and pale yellow for a misty halo around them. And maybe some other colors just in case.

Tash felt shy about being alone with Nathan. If she wasn't going to be not-liking him, she didn't know how to be with him. She dipped the roller and rolled it on the wall. Nathan continued with the trim where

Kevin had left off. For a while they both worked in silence. Then Nathan spoke.

"You know, I've always been jealous of you," he said. "So I think I've been kind of rude to you sometimes, and I'm sorry."

Tash stopped rolling. She sure hadn't expected him to say anything like that.

"I used to think all the time about how much better my life would've been if I'd had Cap'n Jackie around when I was a little child."

Tash was not a little child anymore. She went back to rolling primer across the wall.

"I thought I was too old for magic games and stories when I got here," Nathan continued. "I missed out. I know it doesn't make sense, but that made me kind of mad at you."

Tash turned to put more paint on her roller, watching Nathan out of the corner of her eye. He continued painting around the door with his back to her.

"Do you know how Cap'n Jackie got to be a captain?"

No, she didn't. She'd never even thought to ask.

"When I moved in, Aunt V told me to call her

Aunt Jackie. But Cap'n Jackie said she wasn't anybody's auntie, and I could just call her Jackie. And Aunt V said no, that was disrespectful, she wouldn't have a child calling an adult without a proper title. Although let me tell you, I was *not* a child. I was fourteen years old.

"So they had a big argument about it right there in front of me. Cap'n Jackie said she didn't care about any fake respect, and by God she was not an aunt. And Aunt V said fine, you can be Uncle, and Cap'n Jackie said no, she wasn't an uncle, either. Aunt V went upstairs and left the two of us to work it out."

"Up to the Captain's Quarters?" asked Tash.

"Yes, the Captain's Quarters. You know, after Aunt V died, Cap'n Jackie wouldn't even go up there. I was afraid she'd die of grief. Mulligan was still here, but he wasn't enough."

Tash turned back to the wall. Die of grief? Could people die of grief?

"It wasn't till you showed up that she started calling it the Captain's Quarters and made it home again. Anyway, that day she turned to me and said, 'What do you want to call me?' I didn't know. I mean, I'd just met her. How should I know what to call her? She thought for a minute, and then said, 'You can call me Captain Jackie. Will that work for you?'"

There wasn't much primer left in the roller pan. Tash rolled back and forth, getting up the last drops.

"What did you say?" she asked.

"What could I say? When Aunt V came down, Cap'n Jackie asked if she thought Captain was respectful enough. Aunt V said yes, and that was that."

So Cap'n Jackie was the captain of Nathan and of Tash. Which made them family, maybe, in some kind of way. Tash wondered if Cap'n Jackie had said anything in her letter to Nathan about family. Had she told him that Tash needed him? Was that why Nathan said Theo would be family?

Tash needed more primer in the tray. The can was still more than half-full, and she was afraid she'd spill it. Kevin had done the pouring before.

"Um, Nathan, can I get some more . . . ?"

Nathan turned and saw the empty tray. He picked up the can and poured more in, and they both went back to painting. A few minutes later, the kitchen door banged open.

"We're back!" yelled Theo. "We got some new window glass for the door while we were at it."

Tash followed Nathan out to the kitchen. Kevin and Theo were taking things out of bags—big paint cans and small paint cans, glitter, brushes of different sizes, putty, glass.

"Good job hunting and gathering," said Nathan.

He kissed Theo.

"So," said Tash. "You guys are getting married. Are you having a wedding?"

All three men turned to look at her. Kevin looked at Nathan. Nathan and Theo looked at each other.

"We are," said Theo. "Next spring. Maybe you two will come to New York for it?"

"I think that could happen," said Kevin.

"So." Tash folded her arms and looked up at Theo. "Will you and I be related then?"

Theo met her eyes, tilted his head to the side and thought about it. Then he nodded.

"We will." He put an arm around Nathan's shoulders. "I'll be your outlaw-in-law."

"Outlaw-in-law." Tash nodded. "Okay, that's good."

"Cap'n Jackie always did love an outlaw," said Nathan.

"She did." Kevin held out his fist. "Here's to us. Outlaws all around."

Nathan and Theo stacked their fists on top of Kevin's. They looked to Tash. Nathan's eyes were shiny wet again. That Nathan, he was so sensitive. As Tash reached to put her fist on top, she slipped the other hand into her pocket and squeezed the key.

That was still just between her and Cap'n Jackie.

The author is grateful to Dr. Rika Maeshiro for thoughtful and thorough answers to questions about broken hips, broken spirits, and embolisms. Any inaccuracies are the author's.